I0626459

THE WRONG MAGICIAN

FUNNY CAPERS DOWNUNDER
BOOK 1

JOHN MARTIN

INTRODUCTION

This novella sets the stage for the larger mystery of Mad Bill's Island, and the dark secret that lies at its heart.

The story starts in Hobart in 1974 with the opening of Australia's first legal casino.

William Clarin is banking on a career in politics to prop up his sagging legal practice.

But when he disappoints some gangsters who mistakingly think he's called The Magician because he can make charges go away, he has a choice to make. Fight or flight?

This hijinks continue in the next two novels in the Funny Capers DownUnder series, *Daddy's Great Escape* and *Escape from Mad Bill's Island.*

CONTENTS

ONE
YOU HELP US, WE HELP YOU.
CAPICHE?

WILLIAM KNEW something was wrong as soon as he came back and saw his secretary wasn't at the reception desk. Miss Jones always told him if she had to go out.

When he saw a silhouette through the frosted glass to his left, he flung open his office door.

What in the blazes was he doing in there without permission?

He forced himself to smile when he realised there were actually two men in there, and they were both wearing fedora hats. 'Um. Can I help you?'

The men were enormous. Both wore suits that looked two sizes too small. The one who looked like a stocky ex-weightlifter was reclining in William's leather chair and blowing smoke rings from a cigar. The taller one was standing near the window scrunching up a piece of paper.

'Come in, but shut the door,' the man with the thick neck said. 'It's freezing in here.'

His accent was American. New York. Like he had a bad cold, or perhaps a mouthful of cotton wool. He made a series of O shapes with his mouth, which sent more little puffs of smoke into the air.

This was Hobart, Tasmania, in 1974, hardly the place you'd expect to find gangsters.

But everyone knew the opening of Australia's first legal casino would bring crime in from elsewhere. Sure enough, there had been a sudden rise in large men swaggering around town in dark suits, dark shirts, dark hats, and white ties.

This was why William had put aside his jocular side and attempted to enter politics — so he could apply some serious pressure to claim back law and order. But the count for the Senate seat had finished on a knife-edge and the result now hinged on postal votes. That's why he had ducked out: to check in at his party headquarters to see if the last ballots were in.

Thick Neck scowled. 'I figured you'd look different.'

'Different?' William felt awkward standing in the middle of his own smoke-filled office still in his overcoat. He wanted to cough but suppressed the urge.

'Well, you don't look like no attorney I've ever known. I thought you'd stink of expensive after-shave, be better dressed and be much taller. Am I right that people call you The Magician? Because I gotta say you look more like a ventriloquist's dummy.'

William's voice came out all squeaky. 'How did you even know I do magic?'

'We're reliably informed that you can make things go away.' The American snapped his fingers. 'Like that?'

'Rabbits, mainly.' William studied the man. Did they actually sell that neck size off the rack or were his black shirts all tailor-made? 'I, er, do tricks in my spare time.'

The visitors exchanged looks, and smirked.

The man in the chair looked at his watch and blew out a stream of smoke as if he didn't have the patience to produce smoke rings any more.

He glanced around the desk until his eyes fell on a tea mug, which he flicked ash into. William tried not to show emotion as he watched the mug he inherited from his father being used as an ashtray.

Thick Neck sighed. 'You'll have to do. The boss is due in court soon. Take a seat, Charlie McCarthy.'

William turned and pointed to the back-to-front image of a name stencilled on the glass panel at the top of the door. 'I thought you would have seen my name when you came in. William Clarin, barrister at law.'

'Shaddup and sit down. We know who you are. The boss is calling in your services.'

'You're in my seat.'

The American pointed towards the two empty seats on the other side of the desk. 'Why can't you sit there?'

From the window, William heard the other man protest. 'He can't sit there, Benny. He'll be in my line of sight.' Just then, a flying paper ball grazed the rim of the waste-paper basket beside the desk before falling on to the rug next to five other paper balls.

Benny raised his voice. 'How many times do you need to miss, Luigi, before you get it into your thick skull that even though you're built like him you ain't no Wilt Chamberlain!'

Luigi stormed over and grabbed another legal document from the in-tray and started pounding it into a ball as William removed his overcoat, sat down tentatively, and draped it over his lap. Luigi went back to the window. 'You think I can't shoot over his head?'

'We are here to talk business, goddamnit.'

William's eyes were watery from all the smoke in the room. The last person who had smoked in this office had been his dearly departed father. William thought about opening a window but he sensed these men wouldn't appreciate a blast of frigid air fresh in from Antarctica.

As Benny leaned back further in the chair, his coat opened just far enough for William to get a glimpse of a revolver in a holster.

'You help us, we help you. Capiche?'

The barrister cleared his throat and tried to sound more authoritative and deeper voiced. 'What kind of trouble does your boss find himself in?'

'What can I say? He likes to take the wheel.'

William smiled weakly, and reached over to pick a pad up from the desk. He took a pen out from his shirt pocket and started writing. 'If he was involved in an accident, I'm sure the barrister I'm recommending to you can make that charge go away easily.'

Benny looked darkly at him. 'The boss was very specific. He wants *you* to represent him. Anyway, it wasn't no accident. That other stupid bum was driving on the wrong side of the road.'

William's false smile disappeared. 'You do know we drive on the *left* side of the road in Australia?'

'Do you?' Benny frowned. 'Really?' He shook his head. 'What's wrong with you Aussies? Does everyone here have death wishes?'

'Please don't tell me he killed the other motorist?' William sucked the end of his pen. 'Hmm, now who is the best barrister I know who'll take on homicide cases?'

'Save your breath, Charlie, because the boss didn't kill him — not yet anyway.' Benny took a final puff, and stubbed out the cigar in the mug. The butt made a sssssssss noise as it sank into the dregs of cold tea. 'Both drivers saw each other in plenty of time and slowed down to a crawl. But it was a matter of principle for the boss. Why should he move when that jerk kept coming straight at him?'

'Let me guess?' William rolled his eyes. 'The cars collided.'

Benny cleared his throat noisily and looked around as if he were looking for a place to spit. 'I've seen worse damage on bumper-cars at fairgrounds,' he mumbled through the gob in his mouth. 'Luigi and me didn't have time to lay a glove on him because two cops saw the whole thing and issued the boss with a summons to front the court. And that's why we're here.'

William was trying to choose diplomatic words to tell the gangsters they really did need to find themselves a proper mob lawyer when Luigi cried: 'Fuck.'

When something slammed into William's right ear, he realised he might have heard that wrong. Luigi had probably cried *duck*.

'Will you cut it out,' Benny growled.

'I did warn him it was coming his way.'

'Quit messing about.' Benny looked at William and smiled. 'I'm sorry about that.' The smile turned sinister. 'You know anything about body language, Charlie?'

William clutched his sore ear. 'Body language? No. What are you talking about?'

Benny kept smiling at him. 'In our line of work, I guess it's an important skill. It helps us to read people. Capiche? I gotta say I don't like your body language.'

William inspected his hand for blood.

Benny thumped the desk so hard the cup jumped six inches and landed on its side. The soggy butt landed in the in-tray and streams of cold tea and ash snaked out in three directions. 'Although I can't condone Luigi's behaviour, it does serve as a warning if you're unwilling to help us with this *one little thing*, the next warning shot to the head is gunna hurt a lot more.'

Benny rose and buttoned his coat, and walked around the desk, pausing to spit into the rubbish bin. He looked William in the eye. 'See you in Court Number Three at 2.15. Don't be late. Or else!' He aimed a finger at the barrister's head and pulled it back like he was pulling a trigger.

———

When the gangsters slammed the front door of Clarin and Son, William realised he needed to check on a matter of law in a hurry.

He opened the door to the little archive where the leather-bound law volumes were kept on two rows of dusty metal shelves along either side of the room.

When he switched on the light, a dark shape on the floor revealed itself.

So that's where his elderly secretary had got to!

Miss Jones was lying on the concrete floor right where his father must have died!

She was gagged and trussed, and her dishevelled skirt revealed her black witches britches with red lace trim under that demure grey woollen skirt.

William bent down and lifted her into a sitting position. When he stripped back the tape over her mouth, she cried out loudly in pain. 'This really is the last straw.'

'It's not my fault you have a bit of a moustache going.' William started untying her hands.

She was trembling. 'That's typical of you, William, making light of this. I thought they were going to rape me.'

'At your age?' William stared at her. 'Christ, I thought they were going to *kill* me!'

She rearranged her dress. 'I didn't come in here to be insulted or be a party to you taking the Lord's name in vain. But I just want to remind you that your father would have punched their noses.'

'That's not fair criticism. He never stood for politics in a bid to rid our streets of men just like them. Anyway, do we have to talk about him *here*! Even Father would never have tried to take on those men. Did you even notice the size of them?'

'Nearly everyone is taller than you.' She shook her hands, trying to get some circulation back, then she hoisted herself up using a shelf for support. 'You think I enjoy doing this job for nothing?'

'I told you.' William put a hand on her back and guided her out of the archive room and into the better-lit reception area. 'I'll start paying you again when I can. I'm having a cash-flow problem.'

'And what if you don't even win the Senate seat? How will you afford the upkeep on that fancy house in Sandy Bay then?'

William placed his hands on his hips. 'You mean the house I've been locked out of?'

'James would roll in his grave if he knew how you'd taken this legal practice so downmarket.'

'Will you please stop banging on about my father. You know his death still upsets me.' His eyes widened. 'You think I asked those gangsters to come here?'

'I'm not just talking about them! Do you have any idea about the number of low-lifes I have to deal with? How many daggy sheepskin boots and tie-dye shirts I see each day?'

'Strewth! You think you're the only one! Somebody has to help society's downtrodden people, and keep them out of jail.' He paused and thought about it, then lowered his voice. 'With the exception of Wacko Jacko, of course. I'd be happy to pay extra taxes to keep *him* incarcerated. You weren't even here when *he* called on me last week.'

'Why can't you at least have a mix of clientele like your father used to have? If you had more money coming in, you'd at least be able to cover some of your gambling losses.'

'You know as well as I do, I don't gamble.'

'You go to Gamblers' Anonymous meetings.'

'I go there as a *voluntary legal adviser*.'

Miss Jones scoffed.

'I don't need this.' William turned his head so she could see his wound. 'Can't you see they've made my ear bleed!'

She placed her hands either side of his head and rotated it towards the light. 'It's red, but it's not bleeding.'

'You sure? You must have been in that dark room for a while. At your age, you probably need longer for your eyes to adjust.'

'There's nothing wrong with my eyes. Or your ear!' Miss Jones pushed his head away, turned and grabbed her coat from the cloak stand next to her desk.

William opened his eyes wide. 'Where are you going? I'm due in court soon to represent those gangsters. Someone's got to keep the office open.'

'It's not my problem. I quit.' Miss Jones stormed out the front door.

———

MOST people removed their hats in the corridor before coming into court. William guessed they did things differently in the USA.

He wasn't the only one who looked up when the rear door burst open. He had been sitting down pretending to study his notes, and the police prosecutor, the clerk-of-the-court, the court stenographer, the four journalists in the press box, the police guard and the three strangers in the public gallery looked just as surprised. It wasn't every day three large men wearing fedoras blow into Court Number Three like they have a typhoon at their backs.

The guard directed the man leading the way to stand in the dock at the front and the other two to take a pew in the public gallery.

'Hats off, gentlemen,' said the clerk-of-the-court in the black gown.

The gangsters at the back of the room looked at each other quizzically, then looked towards their boss for direction.

William was not sure how the boss knew what he looked like. But he glanced down from the dock with a look that said, *'can he make me do that?'*

William nodded. First the boss complied, then the two cronies at the back followed his lead. But none of them looked happy.

'All stand,' announced the clerk-of-the-court.

This confused the boss even more because he hadn't been able to sit down anyway since there was no chair in the dock. His eyes followed the magistrate, Mr Rockingham, who emerged from a door at the front of the court and walked half the length of the bench before sitting down. The officials bowed their heads and the clerk-of-the-court announced: 'Sit.'

This time the boss's glare seemed to say: *'What is this malarkey?'*

William broke his gaze by looking down at the papers on his desk again. They actually had nothing to do with the case, but the unusually tall prosecutor sitting on the other side of the big desk wasn't to know that.

Had Geoffrey Brooks-Dixon bothered to crane his giraffe-like neck it would have been easy for him to see William was in fact perusing the photocopied form guide for race six at Randwick. It was true William didn't gamble on the gee-gees or anything else, but it was an image he liked to cultivate in the hope his opponents would drop their guard. Same with his crumpled look.

But it was a waste of effort today. The man William called 'Sticks' — mainly because he knew Brooks-Dixon didn't like being called that — sat there smirking as if he thought the case was going to be a doddle.

William couldn't wait to wipe the smile off his face and bring him down to size.

How hard could this be? William had never asked to become a mob lawyer but now he realised there was something they could do in return. They could provide protection from Wacko Jacko.

He rehearsed his spiel in his head and imagined the accompanying hand movements.

*'These are the facts, Your Worship. **One:** Our American friend admits he was driving on the wrong side of the road, but he was merely driving on the*

side of the road he is used to. **Two:** *It was a low-impact collision.* **Three:** *Nobody was injured in this minor traffic infringement.'*

Mr Rockingham would probably just dismiss the charge and criticise the cops for wasting the court's time. At worst, he'd adjourn the case to be heard at a later date. William would then apply for bail, which would be a foregone conclusion. At the very worst, they'd take away the gangster's passport for surety.

None of this happened.

What happened was the crime boss got off to a terribly bad start when the clerk-of-the-court asked him: 'Are you Giovanni Salvadori Biggi?'

He stuck out his jaw like it he was daring someone to take a shot at him. 'What if I am?'

Then the smarmy prosecutor stood. 'If it pleases Your Worship, I want to submit a document that was faxed to me not 20 minutes ago.'

Brooks-Dixon's Adam apple bobbed as he opened his leather folder, extracted a piece of paper and waved it theatrically.

'I submit to the court an international warrant for Mr Biggi's deportation to the United States where he will face murder charges.'

———

'Take your hands off me,' Mr Biggi shouted as he was escorted to the door behind the dock that led to a set of stairs down to the jail. He looked back over one of the policemen's shoulders. 'What am I paying you for, ya bum?'

William turned around. Since no-one had offered him any money, the crime boss must have been referring to his lackeys. But Benny and Luigi's threatening glares told him he was wrong, and their dark looks intensified when the command came from Mr Biggi. 'Get him, boys.'

'All stand,' the clerk-of-the-court said, after which the magistrate disappeared through the other rear door.

William watched the thugs get up and leave. If ever a door was destined to be slammed, it was that one. But the journalists were right behind them, and stopped the door from closing as they rushed to file their copy. Then it closed softly after the last one.

When the room had emptied, William glanced at the smarmy prosecutor. 'You might have warned me about the extradition order, Sticks?'

The prosecutor scowled back. 'You heard about it about 20 minutes after I did.'

'Don't give me that nonsense. I've never seen so many reporters in here. Someone must have tipped them off!'

'I must say I was surprised when you came into the court. The word I heard around the traps was they had engaged a Queen's Counsel from Sydney. Fellow who goes by the nickname The Magician.'

This confirmed what William had already guessed. He had been the victim of mistaken identity. He turned to the clerk-of-the-court. 'You heard the defendant? He told his men to get me. They'll be waiting for me outside.'

'Hmm, I only heard him say get *him*. He might have been merely asking them to pick up his dog from boarding.'

'You're kidding, aren't you?' William pointed at the door. 'Why does he need a dog when he's got those two obedient Rottweilers? Can I at least leave the court by one of the back doors?'

'You know Sergeant Jenkins locks the door that goes down to the cells.'

'What about the other side?'

'What are you thinking!' The clerk-of-the-court glared at him. 'You can't go into the magistrate's chambers.'

William mopped his sweaty forehead with his handkerchief. He looked up at the tall man. 'It's up to you to get me out of here, Sticks. You owe me!'

TWO
THE BOUNTY ARRIVES

ABOUT THE TIME William was secreting himself beneath Geoffrey Brooks-Dixon's coat in preparation for making the great escape from Court Room Number Three, Captain Christopher Rose was feeling nostalgic up on the bridge of *The Bounty* XIII.

Even if they haven't read the book or seen the movie, most Australians know the story of *The Mutiny on the Bounty*.

It happened in 1789 when Acting Lieutenant Fletcher Christian led a mutiny against Captain William Bligh, and set him and 18 loyalists adrift in an open row-boat.

It is the stuff of legends that the cantankerous old bugger reached safety 3500 nautical miles later.

The Bounty XIII had a new, different story to tell.

It was the cruise ship's inaugural trip to Hobart but Captain Rose knew this stretch of Derwent River well.

He had grown up in one of Hobart's eastern suburbs and had fond memories of sailing sabots on the river when he was a kid. Sydney was now his home base but he had been in Hobart two years before as the owner/skipper of a wooden boat that had finished the Sydney-to-Hobart yacht race. That time he had sailed to the very edge of the city.

This time a tug boat had rendezvoused with the cruise ship at the head of the Derwent and the pilot had climbed up the rope ladder that had been dropped over the side. This is when Captain Rose had relieved the First Officer of his duties on the bridge. His second-in-charge didn't want to leave his post but Captain Rose insisted, pointing out he really needed to go get some sleep after having crossed Bass Strait mostly on his own.

'How come I do all the donkey work, and you do all the glamorous work?' Wallace Christian said.

'You'll get your turn one day … maybe. Right now though, you need to leave the bridge. That's an order!'

So Mr Christian didn't get to see the pilot take the wheel of the red behemoth, which carried 455 passengers. Captain Rose was wearing a freshly pressed blue uniform, courtesy of a less-than-impressed worker in the laundry room who had to get it to him at short notice. He stood next to the pilot and watched the landmarks come into focus as he puffed on his cigarette.

Up ahead he could see the elegant Tasman Bridge spanning the mile-wide river, and snow-capped Mount Wellington looking down on the city.

Captain Rose pointed to a building shaped like a tower on the foreshore. 'Is that the casino?'

'Sure is.' The pilot puffed out his chest. 'Tallest building in Tasmania. 19 floors. You won't get a better view from anywhere.'

Captain Rose stifled a snigger. Call that a skyscraper? Ha! The Australia Square building in Sydney rose to 48 floors. And this ship had docked in cities with far taller buildings than even that.

Nevertheless, he had to admit the casino had a certain authority as it looked down on far smaller buildings. It was enhanced by a green hilly backdrop of natural beauty you didn't find in bigger cities.

It also carried a mystique as Australia's first legal casino.

If you knew where to go in Sydney, you could find an *illegal* casino to take your money — which Captain Rose knew all too well.

He also knew most of his passengers would make a beeline to the casino during their short stay here.

The pilot looked around at him. 'You really sailed here in the

Sydney to Hobart? You weren't crewing on *American Eagle* by any chance?'

Captain Rose took a deep draw on his cigarette, and shook his head. He blew out a stream of blue smoke, and after he had emptied his lungs said, 'No, we finished way behind the winner. We spent nearly five days in a washing machine. Crossing Bass Strait last night was a lot smoother, I tell you, though I have four green members of the crew who mightn't agree.'

He didn't tell the pilot he actually owned the yacht he was on in 1972. Nor did he tell him he subsequently lost it in a wager with a skipper whose boat finished an hour and 23 minutes better.

———

Geoffrey Brooks-Dixon had not inherited his grandfather's bulk but he had inherited both his tremendous height and the thick woollen greatcoat that had kept him warm waiting on the docks for ships to berth so they could be unloaded.

William Clarin counted his luck it was a chilly winter's day, despite the blue sky over Hobart, because the coat Brooks-Dixon removed from the court coat rack was surely his ticket out of here.

'Don't be ridiculous,' the prosecutor said. 'It'll never work.'

'Why not? You could secrete two people under that thing.'

'You don't think they'll notice I've got four legs?'

'Not if you carry me on your shoulders. They'll be too busy looking up. What are you? Seven foot? I'll make you look even more impressive. I know for a fact one of them is a big basketball fan.'

Brooks-Dixon scoffed. 'I've never played basketball in my life.'

'Luigi doesn't know that. I bet he gulped when you stood up.'

Brooks-Dixon peered down. 'Anyway, I'm actually only six foot nine.'

William scratched his head. 'You'd be surprised how tall you can make yourself if you stand up straight. Look at me. I'm only 5 foot 6. I tell anyone who asks I'm 5 foot 9. What are they going to do? Call me a liar? It'd be a brave person who'd risk a slander suit from a barrister for the sake of three inches.'

The clerk-of-the-court looked at him quizzically. 'I would have pegged you at about 5 foot 2.'

'Then you'd be a poor judge. Anyway Mr Astute, we're going to need you to create a diversion.'

'Me?' The clerk-of-the-court screwed up his face. 'Why me?'

'Well, *I* can't do it! Sticks is probably right. Sooner or later, those knuckleheads are bound to notice something is wrong. I'd prefer it if they didn't notice it was my head sticking out the top of his coat.'

The clerk-of-the-court scrunched up his face even more. 'It's not even my business.'

'It'll be very much your business if the outside of your court becomes a murder scene. How will you sleep at night knowing you have my blood on your hands?' He pointed to Brooks-Dixon. 'And his blood — which, by the way, is a mystery to me. I don't know how such a little heart could possibly pump blood all the way up to his brain.'

This comment caused the tall man to scowl. 'Unbelievable! First, you want my help to get out of here? Then you're happy to insult me. Who just outmanoeuvred whom?'

'Don't be like that, Sticks! Look for the silver lining. If they aim with their guns at your heart they'll only get your head, which means they'll be miles away from mine.'

Brooks-Dixon and the clerk-of-the-court exhaled heavily in unison.

'What do you want me to do?' The clerk-of-the-court closed his eyes as he shrugged.

'I'm guessing you haven't got a smoke-bomb in your lunchbox?'

The clerk-of-the-court shook his head.

'Didn't think so. Plan B it is then.'

———

Benny and Luigi had seen some weird things, but when the clerk-of-the-court started removing his clothes in the foyer, they couldn't take their eyes off him.

By the time he took off his underpants, the 12-foot beast (or 12 foot 6 if you accepted the lie, or a tad under 12 foot if you wanted to be sceptical) had slipped out the door and was walking awkwardly down the last steps.

————

William had been sleeping in the office since Nancy had thrown him out of their marital home. But he knew he couldn't go back to the Clarin and Son premises. Benny and Luigi would look there.

His car had been repossessed, so he trudged 30 minutes up Sandy Bay Road — only to discover Nancy had changed the locks.

He pounded on the door. 'Let me in, please.'

'Go away.' He could see her through the frosted glass at the side of the Tasmanian Oak door.

His voice escalated. 'You don't understand. The Mafia are chasing me, and they know where I work. I have nowhere else to go.'

'Not my problem,' came the reply from behind the glass.

'For goodness sake, have a heart. I've only got the clothes I'm wearing. My fresh stuff is back at the office.'

'I put your magic things and some of your clothes in a case in the shed around the back. The case is next to the rabbits' cage.'

'But where will I sleep?'

'Try your girlfriend's.'

'I told you, there *is* no girlfriend. You weren't supposed to walk in when my assistant and I were rehearsing.'

'Is that what you call it? Now you see your magic wand, now you don't.'

'It wasn't what it looked like.' He pinched his nose. 'For goodness sake, can't you open the door so I can come in out of the cold?'

'You should be ashamed of yourself for breaking your wedding vows with a 15-year-old girl!'

'She's 16!'

'And you're 35!'

'Thirty-six actually! If you really cared, you would have known I had my birthday three days ago. But, oh no! If it wasn't for Miss Jones remembering to bring in a cake, the day would have gone completely unnoticed.'

'There's a thought. Maybe Miss Jones will let you into the warmth of her bed? Like she used to keep your father warm.'

William felt a surge of heat shoot up to his face. 'How dare you make up stories about Father!'

'Really? You think I made that up? Ha! You must be the only person in Hobart who didn't know he was playing away from home.'

This is where the conversation came to a halt.

William collected his case and the rabbit cage, which had three rabbits inside, and trudged back towards town. The sun had vanished behind grey rain clouds that had pushed the last patches of blue out of the sky, and he felt icy spits of rain on his face. Flopsy, Mopsy, and Peter Rabbit were heavy, probably quite bewildered, but William felt jealous they had warm fur coats.

His mind raced as he walked.

Why would Nancy make up such a thing about his father? To hurt him more?

No way could he find refuge with his assistant. Not only did she still live at home, her father had forbidden her to have any contact with him. Just like Nancy, Wacko Jacko had also got it all wrong. William wasn't responsible for the bun she had in the oven.

The trip into town took him 50 minutes this time — what with the extra weight and the constant juggling.

When he reached the ABC offices, he veered right and trudged down to the old derelict docks at Salamanca Place, where he was away from the glare of people.

It was getting dark but he could see lots of lights cast from a large ship moored out in the harbour.

The downpour hadn't started but he could see a sheen of wetness on the footpath.

He looked around for cover, and his eyes fell on the boarded-up door of an abandoned Georgian sandstone warehouse.

Using his hands, he worked free three warped planks, which was enough to give him access. He threw in the suitcase and pushed the cage through the gap.

———

It Was cold in the warehouse, and visibility was close to zero. The thick walls kept out the wind and the rain but not the jaw-chattering temperature overnight.

William had left his overcoat back in the cloak-rack at the court, so the best he could do was pull on an old sweater he managed to locate by touch in his suitcase, and cover himself with his thin magician's cape.

Whenever he felt himself sliding into a deeper sleep, a noise would rouse him.

He'd raise his head, sure he had just heard the scurry of little feet, a hiss or the slight movement of one of the pieces of junk that littered the warehouse. Now everything was quiet. Damn those rats. The little buggers knew when to stand still and hold their breaths.

William lost count of the times he looked at his luminous watch during the night.

He longed for the first rays of light to come through the cracks in one of the boarded-up windows.

THREE
ROCK THE BOAT

IT WENT against Captain Rose's low-as-a-snake's-armpit principles to come clean with his employers. But he had fessed up because he felt he really didn't have a choice. He knew they'd get suspicious of him if they heard about his gambling habit elsewhere.

As long as he kept his nose clean, they said they were happy for him to continue in the well-paying job as captain of *The Bounty* XIII.

It probably helped that he ran a tight ship. He kept crew levels just on the wrong side of minimum and kept wage levels low by telling employees if they didn't like the remuneration, he'd be happy to drop them at the next far-flung port.

But even though he was saving his masters a shipload of money, he knew they were keeping an eye on him.

This is why he resisted the urge to join the tour bus to the casino. Shame. After all the overnight rain, the skies had cleared. It was chilly, but skies were blue again and that was always a good omen for him.

Reluctantly, he took up a position instead behind a recruiting desk in a big tin shed on the docks.

The assistant purser was surprised to be suddenly given the morning off. 'This is my job, sir.'

'Run along, Jane, before I change my mind. You can thank me later.' He winked at her. 'If you hurry, you can still make the bus.'

She gave him a look that said: *are you kidding*?

'Trust me,' he said. 'I haven't always been captain.' He added: 'Bet you didn't know I've got a waterbed in my cabin?'

'That must be nice for you,' she said flatly. Careful not to touch his hands, she handed him the folder that detailed the four jobs they were recruiting for.

Bass Strait hadn't exactly been a millpond but the big ship had churned through the night waves fairly effortlessly. Someone on every trip, however, couldn't handle the smell of diesel and a deck that rocked and rolled a little. But normally they were passengers.

This time, four crew members refused to make the return voyage. This meant they had to be replaced in Hobart, which was a pain.

The only good thing was the water-tight contract they had signed ensured if the wimps ever wanted to get off the island, they'd have to fly to the mainland at their own expense.

Captain Rose pined for the good old days when a ship's captain could order errant crew members be tied to the mast so they could feel the sting of the cat o'nine tails on their backs.

The ship was scheduled to return across Bass Strait and sail up the coast to Cairns.

————

At 20 minutes past nine, a little man in a crumpled blue pinstripe suit came through the door carrying a battered suitcase and a cage.

He looked around the barn-like room to get his bearings then approached the desk, put his things on the floor and sat down on an empty chair. 'It says on the sign outside this is the recruiting centre for the cruise ship moored out there.'

'Correct.' Captain Rose blew cigarette smoke at him. The man hadn't shaved or even combed his hair. 'We have some very specific needs though.' He referred to his folder, which was on the desk next to his packet of Viscount 20s. 'Two security guards, one waitress and one —'

'I could work security?'

Captain Rose tried to keep a straight face as he locked eyes with the man, who was at least a head shorter than him.

'What?' The man picked up on the silent ridicule. 'I'll have you know I'm bigger than I look. Your boss will have your guts for garters if he finds out you've missed the opportunity to hire a person with my talents.'

'Is that so?' Captain Rose turned in his chair and pointed through the window behind him. 'It might come as a surprise to you I *am* the boss on that ship.' He pointed to the stripes on his shoulder. 'Captain. Get it? I'm only sitting in for the assistant purser to get inside her knickers.'

'You can't say that!'

'Why not?' Captain Rose looked around to make sure there were no other witnesses. 'It's your word against mine, and who in their right mind would believe the scruffy likes of you.'

'I'll have you know, I'm a member of the bar.'

'That would explain why you look so hungover.'

The little man bristled. 'Not that kind of bar. The *legal* bar. If you must know, I was forced to sleep rough last night. All I'm asking for is for you to give me a break and I won't be without a bed tonight.'

'Bunk.' Captain Rose dragged on his cigarette.

'What?'

'We sleep on bunks on the ship.' The words came out in a stream of smoke.

The little man waved his hands to cut through the haze. When he finished coughing, he said: 'I don't care if I have to sleep in one of the lifeboats. In fact, I might enjoy the fresh air.'

Captain Rose shook his head. 'I'm afraid we like our security guards to be a bit brawnier and a bit younger.'

'That's ageism!'

'What?' Captain Rose looked at him blankly.

'You can't discriminate against me because of my age. You don't get that I'm a barrister, do you?' Then his facial expression softened and his voice changed. 'You said you also needed a waiter. I could do that.'

'You think?'

'Easily! I've even got experience. I worked as a waiter to pay my way through university.'

'And this was when exactly?' Captain Rose stubbed out his cigarette in his ashtray.

'It was only 14 or 15 years ago.'

'And it was on a ship, was it?' Captain Rose examined the little man's eyes for the truth. When nothing was forthcoming, he said: 'I didn't think so. I think you'd find a ship's restaurant more challenging.'

Captain Rose thumbed the paper on his desk to double-check he had remembered it correctly. 'Besides, the requirements are very specific.' He read from the folder. 'WAITRESS, must look good in a cocktail dress.'

'There you go again! Not only have you slandered me by calling me a drunk, and probably given me cancer by blowing smoke in my face, overlooked me for a job because of my size and my age, you are now discriminating against me on account of my gender.'

'Last I heard, that wasn't against the law.'

The little man thumped the table with his fist. 'It will be one day though and then you could be in trouble.' His expression changed. 'Unless … you sign me up and put me on a retainer as your personal counsel so I can defend you if it ever gets to court.'

Captain Rose swept his hand across his face in the same movement he might make to shoo away a fly. He picked up the cigarette packet, opened the lid and extracted another smoke, which he popped into his mouth. He took a box of matches out of his pocket, opened it and removed a match. Before he could strike it though, the little man held up a hand.

'Do your bosses know you have a chain-smoking problem?'

Captain Rose lit his new smoke and sucked the flame into life. He blew the smoke out. 'As if it's any of your business! If you don't like it, I'd say it's your problem, wouldn't you?'

'You don't think it's discourteous to smoke in an enclosed space when there are non-smokers present?'

'You're not trying to tell me you don't smoke? How else do you explain your stunted growth?'

'You know they'll make smoking in public areas illegal one day?'

'They wouldn't dare,' Captain Rose hissed. 'I have rights.'

Now the little man craned his head to look at the folder. Captain Rose could see what he was trying to do. But good luck with that. Not only was it upside-down, the assistant purser had chicken-scratch writing.

'You didn't tell me you're also looking for an entertainer?'

Captain Rose sent another stream of smoke his way. He had underestimated his ability to be sneaky. 'You're not going to tell me now you used to be a singing waiter at university.'

'Better than that.' The little man tapped the top of his rabbit cage. 'Bet you don't know what I have in here?'

Captain Rose craned his neck, and could hardly believe his eyes. 'Are they rabbits?'

'Certainly are. Tools of my trade. I'm well known in legal circles as a very good magician. They call me Bill The Magnificent.'

Captain Rose pinched the bridge of his nose. 'Give me strength! I'm not letting you bring vermin on to my ship.'

'How bad do you want an entertainer?'

'I'm not that desperate. A magician? Spare me! You seriously want me to explain to the ship's owners how one of our first-class passengers met her end? *The ship's entertainer didn't mean to cut Mrs Smith in half.*'

The little man scoffed. 'What if I promised only to pull rabbits out of my hat, do dazzling card tricks, that kind of thing.'

Captain Rose shook his head. 'The last chap was an Italian crooner.'

'And he wasn't any good?'

'No, he was great. He just couldn't handle the swell.'

'There you go. Do you know how many times I've been across on the Bruny Island ferry? And not once have I had to lean over the side.'

Captain Rose put his cigarette down in the ashtray so he could put all his energy into glaring across the table. 'You don't get it do you? We've never had a magician as our main entertainer. Never have, never will.'

'You can't say that. The first time must come for everything. Neil Armstrong and Edmund Hillary would tell you that.'

Captain Rose sighed. 'Tell you what I'll do.' He just wanted to get the persistent little twerp out of his hair, and if he had to lie, well, he had done worse. 'The ship sails at 7pm. Come back at 5pm and if we haven't signed a singer by then, you're on.'

————

As soon as he left the tin shed, William recognised the man coming towards him. That mop of hair, droopy moustache and gold chains around his neck had been all over telly and in the newspaper, and William had even seen him performing at a cabaret on the eastern shore.

He was a wannabe Perry Como, and he wasn't bad.

William's heart sank. He hadn't had time to come up with a plan on how he was going to keep rival applicants away. He knew they'd snap the Italian up right away.

'Well, if it isn't Tony Cappuccino?' He put down his things and slapped him on the back as they passed. The Italian stopped and turned around.

He studied William's face as if he were trying to place it. 'My name's Tony Doppio, not Tony Cappuccino.'

William slapped his forehead. 'Of course! How could I be so stupid? And me? One of your biggest fans.'

Tony Doppio puffed out his chest. The top two buttons of his shirt were undone, which showed a thick forest of hair. 'You wanna me to sign your autograph book?'

'Autograph book?' William looked down at his suitcase. 'Oh that? No, I didn't have room for it with all these legal documents.'

'Scusami?'

'Oh, I didn't explain myself. I'm a lawyer.' He pointed to the tin shed that obscured the view of the liner beyond. 'I've just been to visit the captain to serve some summonses on him.'

Tony Doppio's eyes widened. 'Really! What for?'

'I really can't discuss that.' William frowned. 'I say, you're not one of the passengers, are you?'

Tony Doppio laughed nervously. 'No, I heard they wanted to hire another crooner.'

'Where did you hear that?'

'From the singer who came here on this ship. He knock on my door last night and say he's not going back.' He put a hand on his stomach to demonstrate why.

'That doesn't mean you have to take his place?'

Doppio fixed his eyes on him, then pointed to the sign by the door. 'I don't have no choice. This other crooner is *molto bene*, even though he's not Italian.'

William turned his head towards the recruiting shed. 'I heard he was?'

'He will steal the work away from me. You donna understand how the Aussie bosses will always hire one of their own kind.'

'Well, this is your lucky day.' William looked around again. 'Bet you didn't know this ship has a problem with cockroaches.'

'Scusami? What kinda cockroach problem?'

William pinched his eyebrows. 'I've probably said too much already. Let's just say if you don't mind cockroaches in your bed, you'll be fine.'

'Is that all? Bugs don't worry me.'

'Really? You like to eat them?'

Doppio's face dropped. 'You said they're in the sleeping quarters?'

'I did. But that's only where the dirty little critters go to sleep, obviously. When they're hungry, they go to the kitchen. Did this other singer happen to mention what exactly made him sick? Mysterious crunchy bits in the stew?'

'That's horrible.' Tony Doppio screwed up his face.

'Quite right, Tony.'

'I donna know.' His face shifted to a look of optimism. 'It might be all right once they get the fumigators in.'

William rubbed the back of his neck and exhaled slowly and dramatically. 'Big ship like that? Could take weeks. And then there's the matter of raising the money to pay the fine? Could take months. If you sign on now they're going to want you to sleep onboard, even though the ship is moored in the Derwent River. And they'll insist you eat on board, too.'

'What am I going to do? This other singer is really, really good. And I told you, the show bosses always favour the real Aussies.'

'They shouldn't be discriminating against you like that. I'm a lawyer. I can help you.'

'Is there really a law against it?'

'Let's talk about it, shall we?' He placed a hand on the crooner's shoulder to turn him away from the recruiting centre.

'How far is your office?'

William pointed. 'I'm working at that pub just over there today. Can you give me a hand with these things?' Without waiting for an answer he picked up the cage and passed it over.

'Are those rabbits?' Doppio said, as he took hold of the handle with his right hand.

'Now you know why they wrinkle their noses. Rabbits have an acute sense of smell. They can sniff out cockroaches a mile off.'

'I didn't know that,' said Doppio as they headed towards The Customs House Hotel. He only stopped to look at the watch on his hairy wrist. 'Bit early for the drinking, isn't it?'

'Nonsense! You can buy me a few beers while we talk business. That'll be much cheaper than my normal fee.'

———

When William returned to the shed at 5pm sharp, his breath smelt of the peppermint he had popped in his mouth hoping to disguise the stink of beer.

'You're back,' said the captain, when he approached the desk with a big smile. Captain Rose looked like a man who had a bad taste in his mouth.

'Well, have I got the job or not?' he slurred.

Captain Rose pinched the bridge of his nose. 'The ship's owners will be very annoyed if you're no good. You've got a tough act to follow.'

'Trust me. I could make the whole ship disappear if I wanted to.'

'That's one of the things I'm afraid of.' The captain smiled weakly.

'I take it no-one else applied for the position?'

Captain Rose shook his head. 'The other three jobs we filled quickly. They've already joined the ship.' He stared aimlessly like a man who had lost all hope. 'I don't really understand it. The departing crooner assured me he would line up a quality replacement entertainer, but no-one turned up.' He exhaled long and hard and loudly. 'So I guess you're it.' Then he stiffened. 'Have you been drinking?'

William locked eyes. 'You don't like me, do you?'

'What gives you that idea?' The captain twisted in his chair, like he was uncomfortable. 'Just lay off the booze, make the passengers laugh night after night and we'll get on fine.'

William looked over to the back window, through which he could see *The Bounty* XIII in the distance.

Captain Rose started scribbling something down on a piece of paper with the cruise company's letterhead. 'The transfer boat will be here in about 20 minutes.' When he had finished scribbling, he handed over the piece of paper. 'These are the directions to your quarters. I trust you have no objections to having a single cabin with an ocean view?'

FOUR
ALL ABOARD

WILLIAM WAS SWEATING and puffing as he descended yet another staircase.

He stopped at the bottom, put down his case and cage, and looked at the map Captain Rose had given to him.

This just didn't make any sense. It looked like he was already on C deck and the directions said to take yet another flight of stairs down.

William walked over to the next set of rails and looked down into what was little more than an open hatch. His nose told him he was either headed down to the kitchen or perhaps the engine room. But it was definitely below deck, which was going to make that ocean view hard to achieve. It wasn't that warm outside but hot air was rising from the void, along with the smell of marine fuel, cooking oil and cabbage on the boil.

William used his handkerchief to wipe his brow, then turned the map sideways to see if that improved his outlook and he should really be going up. Sadly, it really did look like he was in the right place. So he went back, picked up his case and cage, and continued down — climbing backwards this time.

These metal stairs were narrower — and closer to a ladder than stairs — and when he turned around at the bottom he found himself in a narrow corridor illuminated dimly by yellow lights on the ceiling.

He banged the walls with his luggage as he counted down the numbers above each door.

He was relieved to finally reach the right cabin.

He turned the key and pushed open the door, coming eye to eye with a bare-chested man who was halfway through putting on his trousers. The bloke was standing between two sets of bunks, and when he spoke a cigarette bobbed up and down in his mouth.

'You'd be one of the new fellows then?'

If he was embarrassed he was half naked, he didn't show it. He was in his mid to late 20s with a muscular build, a wispy growth of hair on his chin and a single earring. 'I just got up. I'll be out of your way in a jiffy.'

William stood in the doorway, perplexed. 'I might be in the wrong place. I was expecting a single room.'

The man shook his head slowly, spraying some ash. 'You must be the new singer?'

'I'm a magician actually.' William plonked the suitcase and the cage down on the floor, walked towards him, and extended his hand.

'William.'

'I'm Joe. We haven't had a magician before!' He held his cigarette in his right hand and shook the hand with his left. 'Is this the old man's attempt to make shipboard discontent disappear?'

William frowned. 'Who's the old man?'

'You haven't been on a ship before, have you? The old man is the skipper. Captain Rose.'

'Oh him? He was the one who hired me.'

'I thought so.' Joe took another drag, then blew a stream of smoke into the air left of William's head. 'He tells all the new employees they'll have their own room. I bet he also told you your quarters were above deck.' He shook his head again. 'Playing with minds is how he gets his kicks. He knows there's nothing anyone can do about it once the ship is underway.'

William looked around the windowless cabin, which was dominated by two sets of bunks separated by just a couple of feet. It was probably painted white once, but now had a veneer of nicotine yellow.

What could he do? The ship was his ticket to safety. But even if he had wanted to get off, by the time he hauled his belongings back on deck, the ship would probably be on the move. He sighed noisily. 'Where do I put my things?'

Joe took two steps and stooped to peer through the side of the cage. 'What have you got there?'

'My rabbits.'

'You're kidding me, man!' He shook his head. 'Are they alive?'

'What kind of magician would I be if I pulled dead rabbits out of my hat?' William made a clicking noise with his mouth.

'I have to tell you: Bob's not going to like it.'

'Who's Bob?'

'He's one of the other blokes sharing this cabin.' He pointed to one of the bottom bunks. 'He's allergic to animals.' He shrugged. 'Bung the cage under one of the bunks and hope he doesn't notice.' He pointed to a corner cupboard by the door. 'You also have one drawer and space where you can hang a couple of things.'

'So who else shares this cabin?'

Joe pointed to the ceiling. 'Bob works as a waiter up in the dining room. Pedro is a steward, so he works all over. And Pierre is a cook.' He pointed to the floor. 'He works on the next deck down.'

William's eyes widened. 'That makes five! And I only see four beds!'

'Relax. You'll rarely see Pierre and me together in this room. I'm a barman so we work opposite shifts, and we share this top bunk.' He patted it. 'You haven't heard of hot-bedding?' He dragged on his diminishing cigarette again. 'I don't know how he gets up there at his age?'

'How old is he?'

Joe stared into the air. 'Hard to say. I do know he's cooked on cruise liners all his working life, and this is his fifth ship.'

Joe shook his head. 'I know even less about the other two blokes.' He pointed upwards again. 'By the time I get home from working in the Insomniacs Bar just after eight, they have all left for work.'

Joe finished buttoning his shirt. 'Well, that's me done. I'm off to breakfast.'

William's reply was drowned out by the ship's long blast of its horn then the sound of the engines trying to start up. It was akin to someone trying to start a car on a cold morning. Finally, the engine spluttered into life. It was so loud! *Chug-chug, chug-chug.*

'Don't worry, you'll get used to the noise.' Joe raised his voice so he could be heard above the racket. 'Until you do, you might want to go for walks around the deck. You can hardly hear anything up there.'

William pointed to his watch. 'Bit late in the day for breakfast, isn't it?' he shouted. But when the engines suddenly stopped, his voice reverberated around the little cabin.

'You'll get used to that, too,' said Joe. 'Stop-start-stop-start. They frequently have trouble getting this old girl started properly. I sometimes wonder if they get the cooking oil confused with the marine fuel, which would also explain some of the food served to staff.'

He stubbed out his cigarette in a saucer he got from the top bunk. 'Not that it's usually a problem for me because I have the good sense to eat above deck.' Joe smiled. 'If you pretend you're one of the passengers, you can get premium beer here at 6am and good bacon and eggs in the all-day Breakfast Club.'

'If it's any consolation, my rabbits don't make a noise.'

'Neither did the fake chest hair Bruce used to keep in a box. But it still made Bob itch.'

'Bruce?'

'The crooner. He called himself Franco on stage but he was actually Australian. Clever bugger also had a stick-on mo, which meant he was able to sunbathe by the passengers' pool with complete anonymity during the day. Even the old man could never find him.'

'From what I hear, he probably spent more time doubled over the rail than working on his tan.'

'Don't you believe it.' Joe shook his head. 'Bruce had lined up work in Hobart. He used this gig as free passage across Bass Strait, and then he got out of his contract by using the seasick excuse. Clever bugger.'

The engine spluttered back into life.

———

When Joe had gone, William spent some time putting away his things under difficult and cramped circumstances.

The *chug-chug, chug-chug* of the engine made it hard to think straight and played havoc with his head.

Nancy had always packed all kinds of things for herself with the excuse you never knew what might come in handy on holiday. Yet she had packed the barest of essentials for him, least of all headache tablets.

What he really needed was a Bex and a good lie-down.

But fat chance there was of that. There was too much noise and too much cigarette smoke to sleep.

Most of his things went under the bunk but he managed to hang up his good clothes, and changed into brown slacks, a brown body-shirt and a beige pullover before going to check out the ship and get some fresh air.

———

He was walking along one of the upper decks when he saw the back of her. She was wearing a little black dress he had never seen before but he'd recognise that wrinkled neck anywhere.

'Eloise? What are you doing here?'

Miss Jones was leaning over the rail, champagne glass in hand, watching the black water of the Derwent River swish by as the big liner finally got underway.

She turned and blinked as the outside lights on the deck half-blinded her.

With one hand on her glass, she raised her other hand to shield her eyes. 'What are you doing here! I thought you were broke?'

'I've signed on as one of the ship's entertainers.' He thought about what Nancy had said. But one look at the scrawny old biddy reassured him his estranged wife had been just trying to wind him up.

She frowned. 'Is this another one of your deceits? You can't sing.'

'Thanks for the vote of confidence.' He gave a little bow. 'Meet Bill the Magnificent.'

'My godfather!' William had never heard her take the *Lord's* name in vain but her dead godfather had come in for a hiding over the years. 'What about your tilt at the Senate? I thought you were relying on the extra money?What if you're declared the winner of the poll and no one can find you because you're at sea.'

'Money is of no use to me if I'm dead. If the Senate officers can't find me, neither will anyone else.' He pointed to the lights on shore whizzing by. 'Those gangsters are probably searching for me high and low in Hobart, which is why I had to take this job to get away from them. You think they were threatening in the office? Let me tell you, they got a lot more angry when I failed to get their boss off in court. You should be pleased to see me still alive.'

Miss Jones made a gagging noise, which made him look around for a cat coughing up a fur ball. When she had finished choking, she said: 'You mean to say I'm spending what's left of my life savings so I could get away from *you*, only for you to be on the ship so you can get away from *them*. This means I'm going to have to watch your crumby magic show night after night!'

'I resent that. My act has won awards.'

'You call a certificate of appreciation from Lindisfarne North Primary School an *award*?' He got a whiff of her lavender perfume.

'The kids always love it.'

'I think you'll find flatulence jokes and disappearing coin tricks will wear thin on adult audiences night after night.'

'Oh, ye of little faith. All I have to do is scale my act up a little. If I can convince people a coin has disappeared, I only have apply the same principles to make a whole person disappear.'

The look she gave him indicated she didn't share his optimism.

'Wait till you see me pulling rabbits out of my hat. That will knock your socks off.'

She rolled her eyes. 'That'll really pack the cabaret room night after night just to see the same old trick?'

William steepled his hands. 'But that's what you don't get. It won't be the same rabbit every night. I've got three of them with me.'

Miss Jones looked up to the dark sky. 'Your father would roll in his grave if he knew what you had done with his legacy.'

'Will you leave Father out of this for once? He would have admired my survival skills. You got off easy. All those gangsters did to you was lock you in the archive room. I'm pretty sure they had a shallow grave in mind for me.'

'You've only got yourself to blame. The firm's clientele isn't what it used to be in James's day.'

William met her eyes. 'Will you stop going on about the quality of my clients. You'll get your reward in heaven. Soon I hope.'

'You never change, do you?' Miss Jones glared back. 'Well, *I have*. The sea air is inspiring me to tell you something I should have told you years ago.'

'What are you talking about, Eloise?' William said it slowly because he had a bad feeling. Sea air? They hadn't even left the river.

'There you go again. Even your father never called me by my first name. Even when we were getting intimate in the dark, he called me Miss Jones.'

The blood drained from William's face. 'Intimate?' He lurched towards the rail. 'I feel sick.' He felt bile in his mouth.

'There! I've finally told you! You can't believe the weight that's been lifted from my shoulders.'

'You mean you're *proud* of being his bit on the side?'

Miss Jones smiled and walked over to a nearby table and refilled her glass from a bottle sitting in a bucket of ice next to an empty glass. 'Oh, it wasn't just from the side,' she said when she returned to the edge of the deck. 'God, we did it standing up, lying down, from all angles and in a variety of places. At work was a naughty treat. We used to play a little game. He'd say, "Miss Jones, bring your stenographer's pad into the archive room. I need you to take some dic."'

William clenched his eyes shut. 'Please tell me you're making this up?'

'Why would I be making it up? Your father meant the world to me. He promised to leave your mother for me.'

'He did what!' William opened his eyes wide. 'I never thought I'd ever be thanking his dodgy heart for taking him away from us so soon.'

She stood up straight. 'Oh, get a grip on yourself, William. There was nothing wrong with his blinking heart. It was that weighty legal book falling on his head that killed him. If they had bothered with a proper autopsy, they might have found the bump.'

He looked at her, speechless.

Miss Jones met his eyes and smiled again. 'Let's just call it his last stand, shall we? I did what I had to do to protect his reputation … and, in turn, your reputation, too, you ungrateful little turnip.'

William poked out his jaw. 'What did you just call me?'

'I just couldn't bring myself to call you an ungrateful little turd.'

'I resent that.' He raised himself to his full height, but when he realised it was still well below her height, he changed tack. 'Oh, I get it now. You're making this up to extort money out of me.'

'Oh, grow up, William. If I thought you actually *had* some money, I would have informed you of your obligations years ago. I never knew how you couldn't have known. It's not like it was a big secret.'

William cupped his head in his hands. 'I thought Nancy was just trying to needle me.'

'Where *is* your wife?'

'You know as well as I do, she's thrown me out. But she couldn't resist one last barb. I didn't believe her when she told me about you and father *yesterday!* I can't believe she's kept this secret from me all these years?'

'Oh, I like her style. Obviously she was waiting for the moment when it would hurt you most.'

William's voice came out like he had a mouth full of broken glass. 'For all I know you got together with Nancy to make this story up just to get back at me.'

She shook her head. 'It wasn't always in the dark either.' She smiled at the memory. 'Most days we left the light on so he could see the gold embossed titles of the law books, which really got him going.'

Miss Jones stared into the night. God knows what pictures were running through her mind. 'He promised to set me up for life.'

'How come you didn't even get a mention in the will?'

'Don't I know it! It hasn't been easy all these years working for you and hoping that somehow you knew James had promised to take care of me.'

He screwed up his face. 'Do you know how many times I've been in that archive room?'

'Oh, spare me! Think of the times you asked me to fetch a book, and how that made *me* feel. To add insult to injury, I've had to work for nothing lately.'

'I told you. I had a cashflow problem.'

Miss Jones rolled her eyes. 'I suppose you found enough money to get that floozie on to this cruise though.'

'Floozie? What floozie?'

'Your assistant.' The shift in her expression told William she had already come to a wrong assumption. 'I get it now. This is typical of your duplicity! You pretend you're escaping those gangsters, but really you're taking her to the mainland to get her an abortion, aren't you?'

'What are you talking about? You *have* been talking to Nancy, haven't you? I'm doing my act *solo*. For gawd's sake, Rita's only 16.'

He felt another wave of feeling sick. 'I'll tell you what I told Nancy,' he said, wiping a hand across his lips. 'The first I knew I was even in the frame was when her father came to see me at the office last week.'

'Did he present some kind of evidence of your paternity?'

'Are you kidding? Men like Wacko Jacko don't deal with the facts. They wake up with a hangover and blood on their knuckles, and use the memory loss as their alibi to murder.'

'You didn't think to face up to him like your father would have done?'

William glared at her. 'I don't think you realise how traumatic this was for me. Jacko had just been released from Risdon, where he had been doing a stretch for GBH. If I hadn't been able to get through to him I was a barrister with the influence to make sure he went back to prison, I probably wouldn't even be here speaking to you.'

'Why would the girl tell him you were the father if it wasn't true?'

William shrugged. 'Beats me. The truth is I never encouraged those Italian thugs but I did come to hope they might be able to offer me some protection, quid pro quo like. But that really didn't end well.'

His demeanour changed. 'Now I think about it though, now I'm safely on this ship I've not only outsmarted the mafia, I've got myself out of Wacko Jacko's reach.'

He broke into a smile. 'I think I deserve some of your champers, don't you?'

'Are ship's crew even allowed to fraternise with the paying customers?'

William felt affronted. 'I don't think you appreciate the shock you've given me tonight? And now you're trying to begrudge me a little of your champagne.' He pointed to the table. 'It's not like you don't have a spare flute?'

'Oh that? That's for my nephew, Christopher. He'll be joining me as soon as we head into open water.'

———

William didn't twig at first exactly who this Christopher was.

It hit him like an acorn falling out of a tree when Miss Jones told him this was her chance to have some quality time with the captain.

'I thought you said you were waiting for your nephew!' William felt his facial muscles tighten.

'I am. Who would have thought little Christopher Rose would grow up to captain a great big ship like this! I still remember him playing tugboats in the bath.' She pointed to a balcony on one of the top decks. 'Wasn't it nice of him to upgrade me from a share cabin to a first-class suite with an ocean view from the balcony?'

William shook his head as he started trudging away. He suddenly wasn't feeling celebratory any more.

Miss Jones shouted after him. 'You'll have to meet him, just not now.'

He stopped and turned. 'I've already met him.'

'He's invited me to dine at his table tomorrow. I'll try for an invitation for you, too?'

The heat rose to William's face. 'I can't. I've got my first gig at 8 o'clock.'

'That's good timing then. Dinner's at 7pm.'

'Can't make it, sorry. I have to practise.'

William walked away, leaving Miss Jones nursing her champagne glass by the rails.

She had lost touch years ago with Christopher and had had no idea what he had become.

Nor had he foreshadowed his visit to Hobart. But why would he? His parents were long dead and his siblings had scattered wide.

She had decided on a whim to join the cruise when the liner appeared in the bay. It would eat up the last of her savings but she had fallen into the unexpected lap of luxury for a few weeks and it would be silly not to enjoy it. She knew there'd be plenty of time to adjust to her new life dependent on the government pension.

———

William had just reached the bottom of the second set of stairs when he turned around and saw them.

The size and swagger of the men coming towards him were unmistakable but Benny's face was turned as he admonished Luigi, who was pretend slam-dunking the low roof of the corridor.

William's shoulders tightened as he ducked under the stairwell.

If the gangsters had looked down, they would have seen him lurking between the rungs.

But they were too busy arguing as they climbed.

'Cool it, will you, Wilt.' Benny spoke like he had something he needed to spit out again. 'We know he's on the ship somewhere.'

'Yeah, but why do we have to pretend to be security guards?'

'The captain hired us for real, didn't he? Come on. Sooner we leave this stinking, noisy corridor, the sooner we'll get some fresh air. You sure you didn't fart?'

Their voices trailed off as they reached the top of the stairs and continued on their way. Quick as he could, William scooted down the corridor, holding his breath. He found his cabin and ducked inside the now-dark room. He slammed the door behind him and fumbled around for the light switch.

———

An old man raised his head from one of the top bunks. His slow blinking told William he had woken him up, though he was impressed he had even gone to sleep with the noise of the engine.

The man sat up, throwing his blanket aside, and stared at William as if he were trying to place him. 'How long have I been asleep?' he shouted.

'You weren't even here when I was in here less than an hour ago.'

'You must be the new singer?' You look like you've just seen a ghost.'

'Not just one — two. Though I suspect it's me who is in danger of being made into a ghost. Possibly an Angelfish.'

The man rubbed his rheumy eyes. He looked puzzled, like he was trying to fathom a dream he had woken up from.

'I thought I was safe on the ship. I can't believe those gangsters tracked me here.'

'Really? Gangsters? On this ship? You sure?'

William tore at his hair and pointed to the door. 'I just saw them in the corridor. They've signed on as security guards.'

The man tensed. 'We do get a lot of odd people sign on as crew. But how do you know they are gangsters?'

'I bet you don't get too many Americans who are as tall as the Empire State Building and as wide as brick shithouses.'

'Oh them?' The man relaxed. 'I cooked their lunch. Kareem and Wilt are the new security detail.'

'Who? Their real names are Benny and Luigi!'

The old man shrugged. 'Crew members use aliases all the time, nothing unusual about that. What is odd is that the lucky buggers were given a cabin all to themselves?' He pointed to the side wall. 'Next door.'

'You mean *right next to us*?'

'No, I mean on the next ship.' The man screwed up his face. 'Of course I mean right next to us. In the next cabin. Last I knew, that's what *next door* means.'

'No need to get stroppy. You don't think they're really security guards, do you?'

The old man shrugged. 'Everyone pretends to be someone else when they run away to sea. What are you pretending to be? A pocket size Italian opera singer?'

'Didn't someone tell you I'm a magician.' William reached up to shake hands. 'I'm guessing you're Pierre. I'm William.'

William then pulled out the rabbit cage from under the bunk, and lifted it up so Pierre could see Flopsy, Mopsy, and Peter Rabbit as evidence he really was a magician.

The old man wrinkled his nose. 'You're kidding me. We've got enough people in this tiny space already. Now you're telling me we have to share it with critters? Bob's going to freak out!'

The man rubbed the back of his neck. 'What makes you think those Americans are chasing you anyway? How does your theory sit with the fact they arrived on this ship about six hours before you?'

William gave him a hard look. 'How's that even possible?'

Pierre shook his head. 'I know for a fact those Yanks came aboard late morning because I cooked them both a steak for lunch. Nice big juicy T-bones, too.'

'You saw them?'

He shook his head. 'Word spreads quickly on a ship when blokes as big as that come aboard. But the only thing I saw is how they gnawed the hell out of those bones. When I sent them up in the dumbwaiter the steaks were fully formed, when they came back even the bones were half gone.'

This tidbit added fuel to William's imagination. 'Oh, that's comforting!'

'Relax. I don't think either of them really are who you think they are. Besides, we have a very high turnover of security men so chances are they won't be on the ship for long. The last pair we had weren't even on here long enough to even discover the ship has its own jail.'

William's eyes widened. 'The ship has cells?'

'Just one cell. But because it's near the kitchen we mostly use it as a place to store our potatoes and all the other vegetables.'

'But not baddies?'

'Depends what you call bad. The captain had four bags of brussels sprouts delivered to the ship in Hobart. He *loves* his brussels sprouts, so he thinks everyone else does, too.' He sighed. 'They're in the cell along with the potatoes, carrots —'

'Carrots! You can't get me some, can you?'

'Why would I do that?'

'Not for me.' William pointed to the rabbit cage, which was now on the floor between the bunks. 'I joined this ship so hastily, I forgot to think how I was going to feed the rabbits.'

'I dunno,' said Pierre. 'We need every one of those vegetables to feed all the passengers. Do you know how many meals we're expected to serve on this trip? I happen to know the captain, for one, loves his carrots, too. There will be hell to pay if he looks down on his plate one night and sees they're missing.'

'They'll be more hell to pay if Flopsy, Mopsy, and Peter Rabbit get scurvy.'

Pierre scratched his head. 'Rabbits don't get scurvy. Do they?'

'They probably do if all they have to eat are toenails.'

'Toenails! Who in their right mind would feed them toenails?'

William looked up at him. 'Didn't I tell you these are free-range rabbits? You'll be all right as long as you don't let your feet hang over the side of the bunk.'

———

William turned in early. What else could he do? He knew the gangsters would be looking for him and he wanted to minimise his contact with the captain, who would probably like him even less when he found out William's father had taken advantage of his dear old auntie.

He stripped down to his undies and singlet, put his clothes away in his little corner cupboard, turned off the light by the door, and climbed the ladder to the top bunk opposite Pierre.

He lay there thinking, the engine below him thumping over and over, and the concoction of smells creeping in under the door and rising up with the hot air to his bunk. Luckily for him, his fitful night in the warehouse had left him dead tired, and he drifted off to sleep.

When he awoke some time later, two people were snoring in the bottom bunks. The cabin air was choked with cigarette smoke and the smells that four sleeping men emit in the night.

William could only hold his breath for so long before he realised resistance was futile, and he gasped and breathed in whatever oxygen was available. He looked at the luminous hands of his watch, which told him it was about quarter past two.

Chug-chug, chug-chug.

Would he ever get used to the sound of the engine?

He climbed down the ladder slowly, trying not to waken the sleeping men. Any creak he made was masked by both the noise of the engine and the person sleeping beneath him, whose snoring sounded like a freight train.

He had to feel his way along the top of his bunk to find the way to his corner cupboard. Bingo! He found the knob and slowly pulled back the drawer, gathered up his clothes and his shoes, felt for and found the cabin door, and opened it.

He closed the door quietly behind him and breathed in deeply. It wasn't exactly fresh, being tainted with the smell of cabbage and oil, but the air was blissful after the stuffy confines of the cabin.

The row of dim lights along the ceiling showed the coast was clear.

He hoped Benny and Luigi were sleeping soundly in their bunks, and wouldn't suddenly appear coming down the stairs, returning from night shift.

It was going to be cold on deck.

He glanced down at the bundle of clothes in his hands and realised straight away there was a problem. He'd never wear a red-checked flannel shirt and blue jeans. These weren't his clothes! He had got these out of the wrong drawer.

He groaned when he examined the shoes, too.

If he had had his wits about him, even in the dark he would have known these weren't his. In the dull glow of the corridor he could see these were at least six sizes too big.

He unfurled the trousers and groaned when he saw them at full stretch.

He looked at the door but realised he couldn't risk going back in and waking the others up.

————

William stood outside one of the first-class suites, and hoped passers-by wouldn't wander by at this time of the morning. He felt like a little tacker who had dressed in his father's clothes and shoes.

He knocked timidly.

'Miss Jones, are you there?' He kept his voice down to a loud whisper.

He saw a crack of light appear under the door and heard approaching footsteps.

The door opened and a monster of a man squinted down at him.

Oh no, William knew that unshaven face.

And Wacko Jacko clocked him, too. 'You!' Rita's father hissed, blasting William in alcohol and tobacco fumes.

If he said something else, William didn't hear it. He was too busy running down the corridor, holding up his ridiculously long trousers so he didn't trip over the legs.

FIVE
HE'S JUST A PICCOLO

AFTER COWERING on the chilly open deck for an hour, William slunk back to the corridor.

He stopped at the doorway and inspected the way ahead until he was certain Jacko wasn't hiding in the shadows. He crept up the corridor, which was bathed in the same yellow light of the staff passage but lacked the awful aromas.

Why hadn't Jacko pursued him?

William knocked on the next door along, hoping it was Eloise's this time.

'Miss Jones,' he called softly. 'It's me. Please be there. Please open up.'

When the door opened a crack and he smelt lavender, he breathed a sigh of relief. 'Thank God,' he said.

She opened the door some more, and he saw she was dressed in her pink flannel nightie glaring at him.

He instantly realised his faux pas. 'I mean, thank your godfather.'

But she continued to glare. 'It must be 3 o'clock.' Without her false teeth, it sounded more gummy than usual. Like "free o'clock?"

'I need a place to stay,' he whispered.

'I thought you had staff quarters,' she whispered back.

'I do. But those gangsters are staying in the cabin next door to our room.'

Her eyes widened. 'My godfather! They're on the ship? You are in a pickle.'

'We both are. If they catch me, no telling what they'll do to me. But I can tell you this. When they cotton on you are on this ship, I doubt they'll want to leave any loose ends, potential witnesses.'

'What are you trying to say, William?'

'*Dead meat* comes to mind.'

She raked her forehead. 'I need to tell my nephew. Christopher needs to know thugs are in his employ.'

'Nooooooo.' William put a finger to his lips. 'If you tell him, that'll blow my cover, too. They'll throw us all in the cell together.'

'What cell?'

'Down next to the kitchen. But there's only one of them. There'd be nowhere for me to hide. The two of them would tear me limb from limb.'

'Well, you can't stay here. What would people say?'

'They wouldn't know. I could sleep on your sofa.' He got up on the balls of his feet, trying to look past her. 'I presume you do have a sofa.'

She pointed to the side. 'It's kind of short.'

'What a coincidence! So am I.'

'What about your young floozie?' She squinted and her voice rose.

'Shhhh!' William gestured with his hands. 'Anyway, I told you already she's not my floozie and I don't even know where she is.'

'See. That's another lie you've told me. I've seen her with my own eyes. She was out walking on the deck with a man old enough to be her father.'

William threw his hands up. 'What? ON THE SHIP?'

'And you wanted me to keep the noise down! The point is you must see a pattern here? She obviously likes older men.'

'Oh, Miss Jones, that *was* her father.' William lowered his voice to a hiss again. 'I had the misfortune of knocking on his door about an hour ago.'

His eyes bulged as he pointed to the next cabin to the left. 'Your directions weren't that clear. It's another reason to let me in. If he hears me out here *he'll* kill me, then he'll let the Americans kill me again.'

'My! You are in a stew! What I don't understand is why you think you'd feel safer living next door to him than living next door to those gangsters?'

'I'm sure they'd find me sooner down there?'

'But won't her father find you up here, too.'

'Not if you act as my lookout.'

Miss Jones looked long and hard at William. 'This is asking a lot of me. What if people find out I am sharing my cabin with a younger man? They might think I'm keeping a gigolo.'

'Don't be silly Miss Jones.'

She looked him up and down. 'You're right. I don't know what I was thinking. If anything, people would think you were a piccolo, not a gigolo.'

William glared at her. 'Thanks. So speaks the woman who had an affair with my father.'

'Well, he definitely wasn't a picco—'

'Stop.' William raised a palm. 'Spare me the details. My point is: you owe me, Miss Jones.'

'I owe you? I'd say *you* owed me. I've spent the last of my savings on this cruise and it's all your fault.'

'My fault? How do you figure that? I never even suggested you book passage on this ship.'

Miss Jones put her hands on her hips. 'If you had a grateful bone in your body, you would have paid for me to come on this cruise. But no, I had to shell out of the last of my savings. Thank goodness for Christopher is all I can say. What will he think if he finds out you're now sharing the suite he upgraded me to?'

'I won't tell him.'

'Well, I don't know?' Miss Jones glanced over her shoulder. 'They might call it a suite, but it's really not that big.'

'You'll hardly know I am here. Promise.'

'I don't know. I'm sick and tired of being used. Your father said he'd see me right, and you've failed to honour his word. Because of that, I'll be on the pension in a few weeks. This may well be my last chance to indulge before I can only afford tinned cat food.'

'Let me come in, Miss Jones, and we'll work something out.'

————

Miss Jones was right about the sofa. It was short; shorter than him even, which is one of the reasons why William didn't get much sleep. One of the other reasons was he knew the maniac next door wanted to rip out his entrails. But the main reason was he was already regretting the deal he had agreed with Miss Jones in return for his sanctuary.

William tossed and turned in the dark.

Why would he have even touched Rita? He was happily married. Well, not happily. Him and Nancy hadn't actually been happy since the third year of their marriage, which is when the money started to run out. The problem was Nancy had expensive tastes and a caustic tongue.

Rita had been one of William's projects. She had been in the audience at one of his charity shows — for the kids temporarily without fathers because they had been banged up inside. Kids were always coming up at the end to ask him to reveal how he did this magic trick or that magic trick. They were mystified how he pulled rabbits out of a perfectly empty hat. Or how he made objects disappear. Or how he correctly guessed the name of a card an audience member had cut from a deck of 52 clearly unmarked cards.

But Rita didn't want to know any of his trade secrets. All she wanted was to become his assistant. What could he say? He was a soft touch.

This new development didn't make any sense. Why would she be next door? Why would her father be next door, too? In a suite? The only reason the man could afford to stay in H Block was because the government had footed the bills. Had he robbed another bank?

————

The last thing William remembered before he fell asleep was hearing faint snoring. What he couldn't work out was where it was coming from. Eloise in the bedroom? Or Jacko in the next cabin?

Next thing he knew, he was awakened by loud knocking on the front door.

He opened his eyes. Daylight streamed in through the glass door, which led to the balcony. He lifted his head and saw blue sky meeting green sea.

Rap, rap. Rap, rap.

Whoever was at the door wasn't going away.

William looked at his watch. It was past 9am.

The bedroom door opened and out stepped Eloise wearing her blue quilted dressing gown and sheepskin boots.

'Goodness, is that the time?' She glanced up at the wall clock. 'We've slept in.'

William threw back the blanket, revealing he was still wearing his getaway clothes, and he threw his legs to the floor. 'Do you know who this is?'

'I presume it's a steward. I told Christopher they could get access to clean my room at 9 o'clock.'

'I thought it must have been Jacko. Or Benny or Luigi.'

'It still might be them.' She walked over to a nearby broom cupboard. 'Best you hide in here.'

William didn't have time to object. Miss Jones pulled him across the room with her eyes, turned him around with her hands, and pushed him inside.

Then she slammed the door and everything went black.

As his eyes adjusted to the dark, cracks of light materialised on the sides of the door.

He could hear voices.

It seems she was right. It was a steward here to clean the room.

It was hard to tell what they were talking about but William knew one thing for sure: it was starting to stink in here.

———

When the cupboard door opened, both men got a shock.

William blinked against the light and saw a large dark-skinned man stepping back. He must have been 6' 6" and 20 stone! He wore his hair in a ponytail and the soft high-pitched voice that came from him seemed incongruous. 'You must be the new magician.'

William stepped and brushed fluff from his shoulders. 'What makes you say that?'

'Easy. You're wearing my clothes.'

'Oh these?' William pinched at the huge trousers. 'I can explain. Pedro, right?'

'We wondered where you had got to in the middle of the night? You had two visitors earlier this morning.'

William groaned. 'Let me guess. Two Americans? The new security officers?'

'How did you know that? Are you a psychic, too?'

William shook his head: 'You don't need to be Nostradamus to work some things out. I knew they'd track me down sooner or later. Turns out it was sooner. Sorry about accidentally taking your clothes.'

'They seemed like nice fellas.'

'That's just what they want you to think. They're really gangsters from Chicago.'

'And they mean you ill?'

'*Dead* more like it.'

'Shouldn't we let the captain know?'

'I don't think that's a good idea. He'll blame me for leading them aboard.'

'Did you?'

'No! I was told they were on the ship first.'

'So you're chasing them?'

William look down at his great big shoes. 'If I was chasing them, do you think I'd be hanging round in a smelly broom cupboard in these moon boots?'

'So how do you explain they came aboard first?'

'I can't. I just know I can't go back to that cabin now.'

'Well, you can't stay here.' Pedro looked around at Miss Jones.

William blurted: 'Miss Jones is fine with it. Aren't you Eloise?'

She nodded. 'Remember what you promised me in return though?'

William wrapped an arm around Pedro's lower back. '*No-one* must know I am here. Can I rely on you to keep my secret?'

Pedro shrugged. 'Well, our cabin *is* getting a bit crowded.'

William pointed to the wall. 'I suppose you clean next door, too?'

Pedro nodded. 'Where the man and his pregnant daughter are? I've just come from there.'

'Well, don't tell them that I'm here either.'

'Don't tell me they're out to get you, too?'

'Just Jacko.' When he was met with a blank look, he added. 'The father.'

'How come? Did you get the girl pregnant?'

William's eyes became dinner plates. 'Of course not. She's only 16!'

Pedro put a finger to his nose. 'That's where you're wrong. Today's her 17th birthday.'

'How do you know that?'

'I told you, I just cleaned their cabin. The girl told me she was waiting for her father to wake up so they could go to the dining room for a special birthday breakfast. Fat chance of that happening though. You should have seen the number of empty beer cans I cleaned up?'

Pedro sighed. 'Poor girl. I guess she just wanted someone to talk to on her birthday. When I told her there were plenty of fun things she could do on the cruise alone, she said she wasn't interested. She said they were only doing the cruise to get to Cairns.'

William frowned. 'There must be cheaper ways to get to Cairns than on a cruise liner. How much would he be paying for that suite?'

Pedro shrugged, and looked to Miss Jones for an answer.

'Don't ask me. I got an upgrade.'

William waggled a finger towards her. 'The captain is only her nephew, Pedro.'

'Seriously?' the steward said.

'So you'd better do a good job of making her bed, or whatever it is you stewards do,' said William.

'I was about to start sweeping the floor. If you don't mind me saying you need to brush up on your hide-and-seek skills. I didn't even

know I was looking for you but the broom cupboard was the first place
I looked.'

'Yeah, sorry if I made your clothes all smelly. You can have them
back as soon as you bring me my stuff. Some of my clothes you'll find
in the second and third drawers. And you'll find my suitcase under the
left-hand bunk, right next to my rabbit cage.'

———

William looked down into the empty cage. 'Where are they?'

'Where are what?' Pedro shrugged. 'I brought what you wanted.
Your clothes, your suitcase and this cage.'

'But where are Flopsy, Mopsy, and Peter Rabbit?'

'You didn't tell me there were supposed to be rabbits in the cage!'

'I would have thought that would be obvious. I'm a magician. Why
would I bring an empty cage on to the ship?'

'Have you checked your hat?'

William closed his eyes. 'God help me.'

Miss Jones's voice caused him to open his eyes abruptly. 'Language,
William! There is no need to take the Lord's name in vain. Especially
over some missing rabbits.'

'That's easy for Him to have you say. If He sees everything he probably knows where they've got to.'

'William!'

'This is a very serious matter for a magician, Eloise. You wouldn't
take a hammer away from a builder and expect him to be able to build
a house.' Then he looked up at Pedro. 'Say, you don't think Pierre has
nicked my rabbits?'

'What would he do with them?'

'He's a cook, isn't he? And he knew about them. If rabbit stew is on
the menu at the buffet tonight …'

William felt pale. 'I hope I'm wrong.'

'Me, too,' said Pedro. 'But we better tell the captain rabbits might be
loose on the ship.'

'Nooooooo,' cried William. 'Why does he even need to know?'

'The last thing we need is for rabbits to chew through some of the sensitive navigational cabling on the ship. Have you ever seen a rabbit plague? They eat through everything. They could make the ship crash on to rocks.'

William shook his head. 'We're talking about three white rabbits here, Pedro.' He did the finger movements. 'Count them. Three. Last I heard, three rabbits doesn't constitute a plague.'

'I still think Captain Rose should know.'

'What can he do about it?'

Pedro shrugged again. 'I don't know. He'd probably re-task those new security officers to catch them.'

William's eyes widened. 'Win-win! While they are busy looking for missing rabbits, they will have less time to look for me.'

Pedro smiled, like he had just won Mastermind.

'Go ahead, and tell him then. But you don't have to tell him where I am. If he asks, tell him the stress I have pining for my rabbits has given me a migraine, which is why I can't do the show tonight.'

'You want me to send a doctor to your cabin?'

'Sheesh! I'm not *really* sick, Pedro. But *no-one* must know where I am? If the captain insists on locating me, just shrug and tell him you *guess* I've found a dark room somewhere.'

'You want me to arrange room service meals for you?'

'Great idea,' said William

Miss Jones looked indignant. 'Well, I'm not staying in to eat. Christopher has invited me to dine at his table.'

'How will I explain the room service meals?' said Pedro as he opened the door to leave.

'Just tell them Miss Jones eats like a pig.'

'William!'

———

An hour later someone hammered on the door. 'Let me in, Auntie Eloise! It's me.'

Miss Jones turned to William.

'Don't look at me!' he hissed. 'I didn't ask him to drop in on you.'

She looked around and dropped her voice to a whisper. 'You'll have to hide in that cupboard again.'

William held up his palms. 'No way. I think someone must have stashed a loaded sea-sick bag in there one time.'

'Do you have any better ideas?'

William nodded towards the bedroom door as Captain Rose's voice boomed. 'I know you're in there, Auntie Eloise. I can hear you talking. TO HIM.'

William felt the blood drain from his face. Panic swept over him as he met Miss Jones's look. 'How could he possibly know I'm here? I swore Pedro to secrecy.'

'I don't know.' Miss Jones stepped towards the bedroom door and opened it. 'But I suppose I have to clean up your mess again. Nothing changes.'

'I'll hide under the bed, shall I?'

She was shaking her head slowly as he passed.

He was shimmying under the king-size bed when he heard the door close behind him.

He could hear just about everything said in the other room.

'Where is he?'

'Who, dear?'

'You know who. Pedro told me he's hiding here. He even told me his hiding spot.'

William heard him open a cupboard.

'I can assure you there's nothing but brooms in there. See.'

'Well, he's here somewhere. I heard you talking to someone.'

William heard footsteps coming towards the bedroom door.

Miss Jones must have stepped in his way because he heard her saying: 'You can't come in here.'

'Why not?'

'A woman's bedroom is private.'

'As captain, Auntie, I have to overrule you this time. This is a legitimate search for an errant employee of this company.'

William heard the doorknob turn and the door open.

'See,' said Miss Jones. 'There's no-one here.'

William watched as two sets of shoes crossed from one side of the bedroom to the other, then he heard cupboard doors open and slam shut.

'How dare you, Christopher! I never thought you'd violate my privacy like this.'

'I never expected my maiden aunt to be hiding a man in her bedroom!'

'Wash your mouth out.'

The feet kept moving.

'What do you know about this man, auntie? I should never have hired him. I knew the first time I laid eyes on him he was trouble. What was I thinking hiring a magician? This could be the straw that breaks the camel's back with my bosses.'

Suddenly his feet were replaced with a face peering under the bed. Captain Rose looked like the cat who had got the cream, only cats don't get big silly grins on their faces nor grasp their hats so they don't fall off.

'Just as I thought, you *are* here.' He gave William a full blast of smoker's breath. 'Looking for your rabbits under there, are you? Or do you always hide in the dark to soothe a migraine?'

As William started wriggling out, he said: 'I can explain.'

By now, Captain Rose had stood up, so William could only imagine his eyes were rolling. 'This better be good. Otherwise when we dock at the next port, we'll have no choice but to hand you over to the authorities.'

As William scrambled to his feet, he held out his palms: 'On what charge?'

'Charges, plural.' Captain Rose counted them out on his fingers. '**One**: Impersonating an entertainer in order to get free passage on an ocean liner. **Two**: endangering the public by releasing wild animals on an ocean liner. **Three**: prostitution on an ocean liner.'

William and Miss Jones cried in unison: 'Prostitution?'

Captain Rose looked at his auntie. 'Well, how else do you think a court of law will view the evidence of a younger man being in your bedroom?'

'Now hang on,' said William. 'I'm obviously better acquainted than you in the law of slander.'

'You joined this ship as a magician, not a lawyer!'

'Can't a chap be both?'

'Why would you work as a magician, anyway, when you can earn so much more as a lawyer?'

Now Miss Jones rolled her eyes. 'He doesn't earn more, believe me.'

Both men looked around at her. William's look said: how can you say such a thing? Captain Rose's said: how do you know that?

William folded his arms. 'What Eloise hasn't told you is she is my secretary?'

'Former secretary,' she said.

William smiled. 'I'd need four weeks' notice for that to come to fruition.'

Miss Jones bared her false teeth back at him, but no-one could ever mistake it for a smile. 'He is trying to muddy the waters, Christopher. He's only on this ship because he thought he could escape from those gangsters.'

'What gangsters?'

William looked towards the ceiling. He had to go with it now she had let the cat out of the bag. 'Why did you hire those gorillas? I would never have set foot on this ship if I knew they were here first.'

'What are you talking about?'

'Do the names Benny and Luigi mean anything to you?'

Captain Rose looked back at him blankly. 'No.'

'I saw them with my own eyes, for God's sake.'

Miss Jones's face contorted. 'William!'

He ploughed on. 'Super-large Americans?'

'Oh, you mean Kareem and Wilt.'

'Are they the names they gave you? I thought I recognised you? You had a big part in *Gullible's Travels*, didn't you?'

Captain Rose studied his face. 'You really think I came down in the last shower? Not that it's any of you business, but I certainly cross-checked their names with their references before I hired them, and I am honoured to have two former American marines working on this ship.'

'You're kidding me? Marines! How many marines do you know with beer guts who smoke cigars?'

'I couldn't fault the written references they presented.'

William's eyes widened. 'It didn't occur to you those references might be fake?'

'If I were you I'd be more concerned with working out how you're going to find your rabbits.'

William sighed. 'So Pedro told you at least one thing we had agreed on. I'm still going to kill him though.'

'I'd like to see you try. Pedro used to work security before he switched to being a steward. He is a very loyal, honest employee who is a very, very good judge of character.'

'Ask him about Benny and Luigi then.'

Captain Rose shook his head. 'You really think I'm stupid!' He smiled. 'You'll have lots of time to work out who's the smarter of us two when you're out looking for your rabbits.' He put on his best Elmer Fudd accent. 'It's wabbit-hunting season for you, my friend.'

'I'm a barrister. I don't have the skills to catch Flopsy, Mopsy, and Peter Rabbit.'

'You're kidding me? That's their names?'

'What would you have called them? Spot?'

'Very funny! But I really don't care what they're called.' Captain Rose moved in closer and prodded William's chest with a finger. 'As far as I'm concerned you're a magician. Not a lawyer on any ship of mine. And you're definitely not Beatrix Potter. You brought the rabbits aboard, you lost them, now you find them.'

'But what if I can't. You'd have to get Benny and Luigi to find them then.'

'That may be so. But only after they deal with you first.'

'You wouldn't really let them lock me in the cell?'

'You know about the cell?'

'Pierre the old cook told me.'

'Did he? Did he tell you we also use it as a pantry so it's not really empty enough for human occupation until nearly the end of the voyage?'

'Phew! I guess that gets me off the hook.'

Captain Rose smiled. 'Yes, I guess it does. But it means I have to turn a blind eye to whatever creative forms of punishment my security men come up with. Being ex-marines, I'm sure Kareem and Wilt will be careful not to leave bruises.'

Captain Rose let that thought hang there for a moment. 'Another thing: Pedro tells me you can't work tonight owing to your…' He made air quotes. '… migraine.'

'I thought you said he didn't lie?'

'Maybe he believed you?'

'But you don't?'

'You signed on to do a magic show and, by jeepers, you're going to do a magic show. Starting tonight.'

'How can I? I don't have any rabbits.'

'That'll be an incentive for you to find them then.' He shrugged. 'But if you can't, you must have some other tricks?'

'Of course. But pulling rabbits out of my top hat is my grand finale, the drum-roll bit.'

Miss Jones's face lit up. 'Can't you see, William? This is our big break.'

Captain Rose came over faint. 'What are you talking about Auntie Eloise?'

'You tell him, William.'

William looked at her angrily. 'You agreed to wait till near the end of the trip, Eloise!'

'But this is destiny,' she said. 'You need a new main act.'

Captain Rose was getting dizzy from looking from face to face. 'Will someone tell me what's going on?'

His auntie smiled weakly. 'William struck a deal with me to become his new assistant. He's going to make me disappear.'

William smiled weakly. He had actually had no intention of taking Eloise on stage as his assistant. But it's the deal he had offered her because he had been so desperate to hide in her cabin after his latest confrontation with Jacko.

———

What she had said early this morning once he was inside and the door was closed, made his eyes nearly pop out.

'I need you to make me disappear,' she said. 'I need my life insurance.'

William had made clicking noises with his tongue. 'I don't know how to tell you this, Miss Jones. I don't really make people disappear. It's just an illusion. And the last bit of the illusion is making the subject *reappear*.'

'Can't you make an exception on that bit?'

'What are you saying, Miss Jones? If the Law Council found out I was involved in that kind of skullduggery they'd debar me.'

'And what is it you think the men after you will do to you if they catch you?'

She let that sink in.

'Don't forget you owe me, William. Because of your father's broken promises, I have nothing.'

'Not this again,' William hissed.

'So you'll do it?'

'Do I have any choice?'

She pointed to the door. 'Of course you have a choice. You can stay here and sleep on my sofa or you can go back out there.'

He gulped. 'I suppose it is possible to make you disappear for good but I'll need time to work out how to do it.'

'Take all the time you need, as long as it happens before the end of the cruise. You make me disappear, I'll lie low for a while, find a way to claim the insurance money, and disappear to the south of France or somewhere. You'll never see me again.'

William rubbed his temples. 'If they find out, it'll spell the end of my legal career.'

'Don't worry, you'll probably have a greater chance of being thrown out of the magician's guild on account of your incompetence.'

She smiled at him sweetly. 'Why don't you call me Eloise?'

'You told me not to.'

'But me being your new business partner now changes everything. If it helps, I've brought my leotards.'

William felt his forehead furrow. 'What leotards?'

'The ones I used to use for jazz ballet.'

William's eyes widened. 'Why would you even bring your leotards?

First, Benny and Luigi sign on before I even knew I was coming on to this ship, now you expect me to believe you had the foresight to bring your leotards before you could possibly have known there'd be a ship's magician, let alone me?'

She got that faraway look again. 'Your father used to come and watch me do jazz ballet.'

'You're kidding?' He screwed up his face. 'He never came to watch even *one* of my school football matches.'

'What can I say? He obviously liked me in leotards more than he liked you in football boots.'

William grimaced. He decided then and there, the only disappearing act would be his own. He'd have to steal away in one of the lifeboats as soon as he could, and leave Eloise, Captain Rose, Benny, Luigi and Wacko Jacko wondering where the hell he had got to.

———

She had trumped him with this new plan.

Captain Rose glared at him, which was becoming a habit. 'I won't let you make a fool of my auntie on this ship.'

Miss Jones touched his hand lightly. 'It's okay, Christopher. I know what I'm getting into.'

Her nephew turned on her. 'Do you? Do you really! I should never have hired this charlatan.'

'I resent that accusation,' said William.

'Now you want to hold my auntie up to ridicule!' By the look of his face, he was turning into Captain red, red Rose.

'I merely want to make her disappear for a little while.'

'And what if you can't make her reappear. What then?'

'Don't you get it? It's just a trick. You've watched too many *Star Trek* episodes. She won't be lurking in suspended animation. She'll still be somewhere in the same room.'

The captain looked Miss Jones in the eye. 'I feel very uncomfortable about this, auntie. I think we need to talk.' He turned on the magician. 'In private.'

'Don't mind me.' William began turning on his heels. 'I'll just go back into the bedroom.'

Captain Rose grabbed him by the ear and turned him back around.

'Ouch! That's my sore ear.' William felt like a fish on a hook. 'You have no jurisdiction to assault me like this.'

'Oh, you don't think so? Well, let me tell you. As captain, I only have to snap my fingers to summon Kareem and Wilt, and I'm sure they'll have ways to make you *really* disappear — without evidence.' Captain Rose released the ear lobe and pointed towards the front door.

'You stay OUT OF MY AUNTIE'S BEDROOM if you know what's good for you. Now would be a good time to start looking for those rabbits. OUT!' He redirected his pointing finger to the cage on the floor. 'And don't forget to take that with you. I don't want to see you again until you bring me those bunnies.'

————

William slammed the door behind him and looked left and right down the corridor. It was empty. But one of the bad fellas could appear at any second. Come to think of it, one of his rabbits could materialise, and when he stooped down to grab it, Benny and Luigi, or Wacko Jacko, might sneak up behind him.

William's brow was sweaty. Absent was the chug-chug, chug-chug of the corridor below deck. In its place was the thump-thump, thump-thump sound of his heart.

The corridor had no natural light, just the yellow haze of the row of lights on the ceiling.

He turned back the way he had got here. That meant passing Wacko Jacko's door but he opted to go this way because he didn't have a clue where the other end led to.

He had gone two paces when he heard the door open. He froze as he turned around, conscious he was smiling like an idiot.

He expected, of course, to see the mad eyes of Rita's father.

But it was Rita, and she looked stunned, too.

'Mr Clarin! What are you doing here?'

'Shhh! Keep your voice down. Your dad will hear.'

'No chance of that.' Rita looked back through the open cabin door. 'Can't you hear him snoring? With the amount he drank last night, I wouldn't expect him to stir till lunchtime.'

'Happy birthday, by the way,' he whispered.

'How do you know it's my birthday?'

'I do magic, remember.'

She looked down at her bump. 'Is that how you got me pregnant? With magic?'

'I DID NOT MAKE YOU PREGNANT.'

'Who's the one shouting now? I thought you didn't want to wake dad?'

William felt embarrassed. 'Quite right. He mustn't know I'm here.'

'But why *are* you here?' She put her hands on her hips.

'If you must know, I'm the ship's entertainer.'

'I didn't know you could sing?'

William rubbed his temples. 'Why does everyone just assume a ship's entertainer has to sing? You of all people ought to know a magician can be just as entertaining.'

'They're paying you!'

'Of course they're paying me. I'm on the crew.'

Her jaw dropped. 'And you're doing this without me?'

William backed towards the wall of the corridor, so he could see both ways. 'I didn't think you'd mind? You being in the state you are.'

'I can't believe you dumped me. Wait until I tell dad.'

'He doesn't need to know!' William said it quickly then put a finger to his lips. He suddenly realised he had another problem. What if Wacko Jacko saw him performing in the cabaret room?

Rita looked at the door behind her again. 'He discovered something called the Insomniacs Bar last night. Heaven knows what time he got in? How he managed to stagger home to the correct cabin is a miracle.'

'He didn't mention he saw anything a bit, um, strange when he got in?'

'I haven't spoken to him. I woke up briefly when he came in. Well, it's hard to stay asleep with all that crash, bang and opening of doors, followed by such loud snoring.'

'Yes, no wonder he got early parole from Risdon. No-one probably wanted to share a cell with him.'

'That's a terrible thing to say! He got early parole because he was well behaved. I thought you of all people would cut him some slack.'

'Do you realise the trouble you've got me in by telling him I'm the father of your baby?' He pointed to her bump.

'You know dad? He suspects any man who's ever talked to me.'

'Well, can't you tell him it couldn't possibly have been me? Even my wife suspects I'm some kind of child molester.'

'Is that what you think I am? A child?' Rita straightened up to her full height, which more than matched his.

'I never touched you. I don't deserve to be maligned and threatened.'

'It doesn't matter anyway. Dad knows someone in Cairns who will get rid of it for me. That's why we're on this cruise.'

'You know abortion is illegal?'

She shrugged. 'Since when has that worried dad?'

'What I don't get: why didn't you just fly to Cairns? It would have been a lot cheaper.'

Rita shrugged again. 'Dad says he's come into some money, but they'd be keeping an eye out for him at airports.'

William rolled his eyes. 'What's he done now?'

'Mr Clarin!'

'Don't Mr Clarin me.'

'As if he'd tell me anyway.' She shrugged again. 'He might have won the money at the casino.'

William checked the corridor left and right again. It'd be just his luck for Benny and Luigi to come swaggering from the darkness.

'Is your wife with you?'

William didn't expect this question. 'What? No. She's not talking to me.'

'Why not?'

'You know why not.' He didn't mean to screech like a parrot.

'Oh, that? Sorry. So you're here alone?'

'Look, I'd really love to stay chatting but I'm on a bit of a mission. I've got to track down Flopsy, Mopsy, and Peter Rabbit.'

'Where are they?' She peered into the empty cage.

'If I knew that I wouldn't have to have a new assistant.'

'You've *replaced* me *already*!'

'It was never my intention. But it's Miss Jones, my secretary.'

'Eeeew. Her? That old lady must be 90!'

'She's only 76 actually.'

'I'd like to see you make *her* pregnant. Eeeew.'

'There you go again. I DID NOT MAKE YOU PREGNANT.'

'Well, someone did.'

'Sheesh! Can't you work out who it was? Why do you have to be so obtuse?'

'What does that word even mean?'

'Difficult.'

Rita pouted. 'Well, you do have a reputation.'

'THAT YOU GAVE ME!'

––––––

William gritted his teeth because he knew exactly where he had to go. He guessed the hungry rabbits must have smelt all the yummy vegetables down in the larder, and that's where he'd find them.

He backed down the steps that led to the staff quarters, and crept past Benny and Luigi's door to the other end of the corridor.

When he laid eyes on what faced him now, he gulped. To get to the next floor down he had to climb down a ladder. Not half stairs/half ladder like the one he had just scrambled down to get on to this corridor. This was a proper vertical ladder. Worse, he had to climb down while holding the cage.

He leaned over the rail and peered into the black hole. He could see the bottom, but only just. It was a very long ladder.

He wondered how his rabbits would have even managed to get down there.

He thought about chickening out but when he looked back up the corridor he realised he was running out of luck with not running into the Americans.

So he turned around, closed his eyes, and backed over the side.

He counted 20 rungs as he went down with his eyes and bum-cheeks clenched.

Boy, was it good to plant both feet on firm floor again. He couldn't see what he was now standing on but it felt spongey, like rubber matting.

The yellow lights that lit the corridors above were even dimmer here, and his eyes needed time to adjust to the reduced light.

But he could see he was at a T junction: he could go left or right. But which way should he go?

The engine was also louder down here and the *chug-chug, chug-chug* made it hard to think clearly. On top of this was the smell. He had never realised cabbage smells came in degrees, but it was definitely much stronger down here, which was another sensory disruptor.

When he heard the clatter of pots and pans, he set off towards that noise.

But when a silhouette came around the corner, his heart skipped a beat. It skipped another beat when he saw the glint of the meat cleaver.

It was too late for William to duck into a doorway. The man in the tall chef's hat was bearing down on him.

'Well, look who we have here?' Pierre came to a halt.

'Oh, it's you?' William wiped his brow with a hand. 'You scared me half to death.'

'Where'd you get to last night? Did you steal Pedro's clothes?'

'Of course I didn't steal them.' William raised his voice like he was making an objection in court. 'I got mixed up in the dark.'

'Did you just? I guess you got mixed up some more. Are you lost now?'

William lifted his cage. 'I'm looking for my rabbits. Turns out they've done a bunk from under the bunk.' William examined Pierre's eyes (well, as well as you can in a dark walkway) for clues that he knew something about their disappearance.

Pierre picked up on it. 'You don't think their disappearance is down to me, do you?'

'You and Joe were the only people who knew they were there. I hardly think a bartender would have any use for them.'

'And you think I would? I would never hurt a living thing.'

William glanced down at the meat cleaver in Pierre's hand.

Pierre lifted the cleaver a little and half-rotated it in his hand. 'This? Oh no, this is strictly vegetarian. It's only ever been used to cut fruit and veggies. I was on the way to the larder to cut me some corn.'

'That's what I was trying to find, too.' William spoke breathlessly. 'You said the jail was next to the kitchen?'

'No, I said it was *near* the kitchen.' He raised the cleaver and used it as a pointer. 'It's on the other side of the ladder.'

'Careful!' William saw the glint go past the side of his face. 'That ear has already come in for punishment?'

'It was nowhere near your ear.'

'I'm betting the larder is where my rabbits will be. If they haven't died of asphyxiation. I thought the stink was bad upstairs!' William stepped aside. 'Lead the way.'

It only took them a jiffy to reach the jail / larder.

If William had turned left instead of right at the ladder, he couldn't have missed it.

The passage came to a big open doorway.

They had to step over a raised step to get through it. A strip of heavy rubber went all around the inside of the door frame.

On the other side was a cavernous room with metal walls and ceiling, with a floor covered with more black rubber matting.

At the far end of the room, a basketball hoop hung from the metal wall.

To the left side of the room was the jail.

'What is this place?' William's voice echoed.

'It's one of the first lines of defence if we ever spring a leak.' Pierre pointed back to the thick door which was held magnetically to the wall on the inside.

'This room would hold a lot of water. If ever they close that door, we're never allowed to open it. I forget what force of water it'll withstand, but it's a lot, so you wouldn't want to be standing on the other side if you opened it.' He shook his head.

'So, this is a jail within a jail?'

'It's mostly used as a larder these days. And a recreation room. I don't know what happened to the table tennis table we used to have down here.'

He pointed to the rack of weights in the corner. 'Some of the young posers come down here to work on their muscles. We also get the odd Yank crew member who likes to shoot hoops.'

They stopped in front of the cell.

In his line of work, William had seen the outside and inside of plenty of cells. He had never seen one so brimming with greenery other than mould though.

The cell was filled with boxes of leafy vegetables and lumpy sugar bags probably filled with potatoes. The toilet in the corner wouldn't have afforded much privacy for inmates but the turnips stacked on top of the lid didn't seem to mind.

'You were right.' Pierre pointed to the rabbits feasting on a bunch of carrots they had dragged out of one of the boxes.

William closed his eyes slowly. 'You think?'

Pierre walked over to a hook on the wall, from which he removed the key, before returning to the cell door to unlock it.

'Cheer up! I thought you'd be happy to find your rabbits safe and sound.'

'I would be … if they were my rabbits.'

'What are you talking about? Where else would these white rabbits have come from?'

William shrugged. 'I have no idea. I can tell you though I only bought three rabbits aboard.'

He pointed from rabbit to rabbit munching on their snacks. Count 'em: one, two, three … four.'

SIX
GONE TO THE DOGS

CAPTAIN ROSE BEGGED Auntie Eloise not to lower herself to becoming a magician's assistant.

William had been gone 20 minutes in search of his rabbits, and they were standing in the middle of her cabin still arguing.

'This is something I have to do, Christopher. Can I let you in on a little secret? William has promised to make me disappear for good.'

'For good! How? No, why? Wait. Why are you even telling me this?' He stood with his hands on his hips.

Her upper lip quivered. 'If I go missing, like really missing, like presumed lost at sea, I'm going to be able to claim my life insurance.'

'Auntie! You must have lots of money! That big house you lived in when I was a boy must be worth a fortune now.'

She shook her head. 'That house was taken back by the bank years ago. And I've ploughed most of the little money I've earned into insurance premiums.'

'Oh great! So you've been planning this for a while. On *my* ship! How could you?'

'I didn't know it was *your* ship until I got on here. And besides I never planned to go missing on the ship. I planned to be eaten by a crocodile near Cairns.'

Captain Rose shut his eyes slowly.

'Not for real, silly. My godfather! I planned to book one of those crocodile-viewing boat tours, and sneak away from the group. I would have loved to have seen their faces when they did a head count at the end.'

Captain Rose opened his eyes again and shook his head. 'I'll be the one losing my head at the end of this voyage when we confirm you're missing. Have you even thought this through? How will you be able to claim a cent when you're in hiding?'

'That's where you could help, since you're my closest living relative.'

Captain Rose held up outstretched hands. 'I don't need this right now. I didn't want to have to tell you this, but I'm on thin ice with my employers already. I've had a bit of bad luck with the greyhounds.'

'And your employers know about this?'

'I'm not a fool! I know they are watching me, waiting for the first excuse to sack me.'

Miss Jones tugged at a lock of hair above her right ear, and exhaled wearily. 'You are so very wrong, Christopher.'

Captain Rose looked puzzled. 'You don't think they'll sack me if they get a chance?'

'No, you're wrong about not being a fool. I knew betting on tugboats would end in tears one day.'

He scowled. 'I never bet *actual* money. It was a figure of speech. *I bet the red boat will get to the end of the bath first*. For God's sake.'

She waved her finger at him. 'You're not too big for me to wash out your mouth with soap and water, young man! I can't believe you'd even bet on greyhounds!'

'I didn't have much choice. I've been warned off every racecourse in Sydney.'

'But the dogs, my godfather!'

'I had a good tip, OK? And if she had come home like she was supposed to, I could have saved my house.'

Auntie Eloise's eyes widened. 'You lost your house!'

'And my holiday house! And my car!'

'What did your wife say?'

'She left me a goodbye note.'

'She left you!'

'And she took the kids.' Captain Rose had a dead sound to his voice.

Miss Jones reached out and touched his cheek lightly. 'Oh Christopher. I'm so sorry. It doesn't matter what he's done, a man shouldn't be deprived of his family.'

'It's OK. They weren't my kids anyway. It was her second marriage.'

'What will you do now?'

'What can I do? Even if I keep my nose clean, I'll be working until I'm 90 to pay off my debts. If I lose this job, I might as well kill myself.'

'Don't talk like that. Can't you see, I am now in a position to help you. Who better than the captain to hide me?'

'Oh great. If losing a passenger is enough to put me on the verge of losing my job, being involved in your disappearance will really seal the deal.'

'What will you care about getting the sack? Do you know how big my insurance pay-out would be? I'd split it with you 50-50.'

'You'd do that?' He felt a surge of adrenalin, like the buzz he always got when he was put on to a certain winner. 'Really? We haven't even been in touch for so long.'

'No, but once family, always family. If you like, I can get William to draw up the papers to declare you as my next of kin.'

Captain Rose bared his teeth. 'Do you really think he'd do that? My guess is you two have a pre-existing arrangement. He's probably expecting a large chunk of money, too. We can't all get 50 per cent.'

'Leave that to me. It's high time I got my own back on that little wanker.'

'Auntie! Language!' He stared at her.

'Let's sit down and work out what we're going to do.'

That's what they did.

For the next hour they sat down and nutted out their plan.

———

William stood at the bottom of the ladder and looked up. His arms ached from carrying the cage from the cell. It was amazing the difference one extra rabbit made.

'You want me to take it up?' Pierre said when William puffed out his cheeks.

'No, I don't.' William watched him put the cleaver and armful of corn kernels down on the floor. Did he really think that ridiculous tall white hat gave him mystical powers of strength and balance? 'I'm not having your death on my conscience.'

Pierre shook his head. 'I've come down that ladder with a side of beef on my shoulder. Taking four rabbits up would be easy.'

William shook his head.

'You said it yourself,' Pierre said. 'The old man's going to want to see rabbits. He doesn't know what they look like, does he?'

'No, but he knows there are only supposed to be three of them. I even told him their names: Flopsy, Mopsy, and Peter Rabbit. I'm pretty sure he'll notice there are now four of them.'

Pierre mopped his brow. 'That's a bit of luck then.'

William looked at him blankly. 'Luck? How do you figure that?'

Pierre smiled. 'He'll just think he misheard you when you present him with Flopsy, Mopsy, Peter, AND Rabbit.'

'Who would call a rabbit just Rabbit.'

'Have you got a better idea?'

'No, but it's hardly going to matter if I can't get the rabbits I have got up this ladder.'

Pierre grabbed for the handle of the cage. 'For crying out loud, let me do it.'

William brushed his hand away. 'No! What if you drop them? Rabbits are very sensitive. Even if the fall didn't kill them, they'd probably die of fright. Ditto if they see your silly hat. They'd pop their clogs immediately.'

Pierre looked hurt. 'What do you care? You said it yourself. They're not your rabbits.'

'It doesn't mean I don't have a heart. They're in *my* cage now. I feel responsible for them.'

'We have to get them up there somehow.' Pierre scratched his head.

William looked up at the ladder again and shook his head. 'I can't believe your union even allows this.'

'What union? The old man doesn't allow union workforces on his ship.'

William pinched his nose. 'Don't tell me this is the way you get the food upstairs?'

'Of course not. We use the dumbwaiter for that. A real waiter takes it out at the other end and delivers it to the tables.'

William brightened. 'That's how we'll get the rabbits up there then. We'll put the cage in the lift.'

'I dunno. The Maître d' didn't see the humour in it when we sent a kitchen boy up a while ago.'

'It must be a big lift?'

'He's a very small kitchen boy.'

'He must be bigger than four small rabbits?'

'I dunno …' Pierre's voice trailed off.

'But we can try, right?'

'George, the head chef, is vigilant when it comes to putting things in that lift now. He has to be. The Maître d' nearly ripped him a new one last time.'

'But he can't stand guard all the time, right?'

————

The control panel for the heater was in the corridor outside the kitchen. The plan was to turn up the heat high, George would gulp lots of water and eventually have to dash for the dunny.

'I'll need a place to hide with the cage.' William looked around the poorly lit corridor. The narrow walkway didn't appear to offer any hiding places.

'Why do you need to hide?' Pierre asked.

'We don't want him to see me when he rushes out to go to the loo.'

Pierre shook his head. 'The toilet cubicle is inside. George will never know you're even out here.'

William blew out his cheeks. 'That's good news then. When he leaves the room, you come out and get me so we can load the cage in the lift. How long does it take to get up there?'

'Ten, 15 seconds.'

'I'll need more time than that! You'll need to give me time to get up the ladder, run down the corridor, get up two flights of stairs and into the dining room. I'll need time to create a diversion, too, so I can empty the lift without being seen. I'll need you to draw me a rough map of the layout.'

Pierre picked up the cleaver and the corn from the floor, and went through the swinging door.

When he returned a minute or so later with a pad and pencil, he had sweat pouring off his face as he squatted and started to draw. 'Boy, it's getting hot in there.'

When he stood back up, he tore the top sheet off the pad and handed it over.

William studied it. He was mightily impressed. A draftsman couldn't have done better. The map of the room looked marvellously proportioned and there were x's that denoted points of interest. *Entrances here and here. Maître d' stands here. Lift is here.*

'This is great work, Pierre.'

'Thanks.' The chef grinned bashfully and mopped his forehead with his handkerchief. 'I reckon it'd be even more detailed though if I'd ever been up there.'

William rubbed his temples. 'What do you mean! You must have seen it some time?'

'Keep your voice down.' Pierre lowered his voice to a whisper. 'How would I have seen it? We send all the cooked food up in the dumbwaiter. But how wrong could the map be? The lift must be on the right-hand side of the room if the dining room is aligned with the kitchen.'

'But is it?'

'Is it what?'

'Is it aligned to the kitchen?'

Pierre shrugged.

William pointed to the x that marked the position of the Maître d' and gasped. 'How do you know that's even right?'

'Easy. A Maître d' always stands at the front of the room so he can see everyone.'

'But how do you know this is the front of the room if you've never been in there?'

'Well … if it's aligned to the kitchen—'

'Will you quit it. You have no idea if it's aligned to the bloody kitchen.'

'There's no need to swear. You want everyone to hear? You're the one who asked me to draw the map. You never bothered to ask me if I was qualified to do it.'

William bumped the back of his noggin on the wall harder than he meant to when he threw back his head. 'All I know for sure are where the doors are.'

'Ah, that …?' The chef's voice dropped.

William rubbed his head. 'You're not going to tell me those x's are fictional, too?'

Pierre nodded. Then he shook his head. 'Ask me to whip up a soup or stew, and you've come to the right man. But my skillset only goes so far.'

William looked at him in disbelief. 'How many years did you say you've been on this ship?'

'I don't think I did. But it's eight.'

'Eight years! And you don't know where the doors are to the dining room. Unbelievable.'

'I've never needed to know? I always have my meals down here. Captain Rose doesn't like us fraternising with the passengers. Unless we're launching the lifeboats.'

'Good job you know where they are then.'

Pierre gave him a blank look. 'I have to be getting back to the kitchen. I said I was going out to the corridor for a smoke.'

He disappeared back through the swinging doors.

———

Half an hour later, the door swung back open.

But it wasn't Pierre who came through them. It was a shorter man made taller by his chef's hat. He had a sweaty, red face.

'You'd be the man come about the rabbits,' he said as he brushed past. 'Can't stop. I can't wait in the queue any longer.' As he hurried along the corridor, he shouted: 'Talk to Dennis.'

Ten seconds later, the door flung open again. This time it was Pierre.

'Quick,' he said. 'Bring the cage in here. I don't know how long we've got? His cabin is right by the top of the ladder.'

William stood there and frowned. 'Was that your boss who just went past me?'

Pierre nodded.

'Who's Dennis?'

'That would be me, Pierre Dennis. George always calls me by my surname. I think he suspects the French accent I bung on in the kitchen isn't real.'

'You talk in a French accent? Really?'

Pierre shrugged. 'They wanted a genuine Cordon Bleu chef.'

William massaged his temples. 'He said to talk to you about the rabbits. Do you have a lot of people coming to your ship's kitchen with livestock?'

'You'd be surprised. But quick. Come inside. No telling when he'll be back.' Pierre turned and pushed through the door.

William followed. The first thing that struck him was the heat. Then he saw a dozen or so unmanned saucepans bubbling away.

'I thought there'd be more people.'

'The rest of them are queued up outside our one-and-only dunny.' Pierre pointed to an internal doorway. 'Through there.'

William walked over to the dumbwaiter and hoisted the cage to the ledge. Pierre lifted the door and he tried to slide in it.

The cage was too big!

'I thought you said you got a whole person in here? What was he? A contortionist?'

'I told you. He's a very small kitchen boy. He's only 11.'

'Eleven years old!' William screwed up his face. 'You know there are laws prohibiting child labour?'

'Tell that to Captain Rose. I think he's found a loophole. He doesn't actually pay him.'

William tried turning the cage around. To no avail. He turned it again. And again. And again, which is when he realised he was back where he started.

'Can you hurry up.' Pierre was sweating even more. 'Someone is sure to come back any second.'

'The blasted thing won't fit. I'm going to have to put the rabbits in one by one.'

Pierre buried his head in his hands. 'There's going to be a trail of rabbit poo. George will kill me!'

'George won't even know.' William opened the top of the cage and lifted out the first of the rabbits. 'You can clean up the evidence when the lift returns to you.'

One by one, he transferred the other three rabbits into the lift, opening and shutting the glass door quickly each time.

'There,' he said when the job was done. 'How long do you think it'll take me to get upstairs?'

'No more than two or three minutes.'

William looked at his watch. 'Better wait 20 minutes more till you send the lift up then. I need some extra time to check out the actual layout, create a diversion and get to the dumbwaiter to take delivery.'

'I could lose my job for this. How do you know this is going to work?'

'Relax. I've got this. The rabbits are locked and loaded. What could possibly go wrong?'

———

William got to the ladder in quick time. Unfortunately, someone was coming down.

The black-and-white checked trousers told him he was looking at George's bottom.

When the hat came into view, this was confirmed.

When George reached the bottom, he turned and got a fright to see William standing there. 'You! Still here then? Did you talk to Dennis?'

'I did.' William pointed to his cage. 'He wasn't interested though.'

'Really?' George couldn't have known in this murky light the cage was empty. 'You were probably asking too much for them. You'll be back. This is a long voyage.'

———

William smiled politely and started climbing the ladder. It wasn't easy but it sure was more manageable with an empty cage. He commended himself for having the brainwave about the dumbwaiter. The rabbits would probably enjoy it, too. It'd be like a fun-park ride for rabbits.

As he climbed, though, a new thought came into his head.

Would there be enough air in the lift for them to breathe for all that time? Captain Rose probably expected to see live rabbits.

This thought disappeared when he reached the top of the ladder and stretched his neck past the top to look down the corridor.

Who should be stepping out of their room but Benny and Luigi!

Benny was wearing an Hawaiian shirt and Luigi was wearing a Los Angeles Lakers shirt with No. 13 on the back. His cap was on back-wards. Surely, they would have been supplied with uniforms? Or perhaps they were going out to work undercover? Maybe they were expected to mingle with the guests incognito.

This was a delay William didn't need. Now he'd have to wait for them to leave.

Only they didn't.

William could hear the strike of a match and smell puffs of cigar smoke.

'Where do you think he might be, Benny?' Luigi's voice echoed in the corridor.

'Don't call me that. You want everyone to hear. It's Kareem, you stupid fuck.'

'Sorry, Benny.'

William didn't have to see Luigi's beaming smile. He could nearly hear it. Then he heard something else. *Boing, boing, boing.*

Benny confirmed Luigi was bouncing a basketball. 'Didn't I tell you to leave that thing in the cabin? What's the captain going to say?'

'We're meeting him? Where?'

'He told me if he's not on the bridge, he'll be having breakfast. But you can't take a basketball into the dining room.'

'I thought it would help confirm our cover!'

'You're kidding me! No-one in Australia knows who Wilt and Kareem even are. As far as they're concerned we're ex-military. We're supposed to know 100 ways to hurt people without leaving bruises. I'm pretty sure bouncing a basketball on their heads would leave bruises, don't you?'

William heard the click of a door and the fading *bounce, bounce, bounce* of the ball. Then he heard another click, and the bouncing noise disappeared.

'So what now?' said Luigi.

'Shaddup, I'm thinking.'

———

Benny obviously thought he did his best thinking while he was puffing on his cigar and leaning on a wall.

The acrid smoke added greatly to the cocktail of smells in the corridor, and the empty cage grew heavier as he held it.

By the time Benny and Luigi finally moved on, William could barely wait to get to where he could breathe freely. He counted to a hundred to let them distance themselves, then dashed down the corridor coughing and gasping. When he reached the top of the stairs, he put the cage down on the deck and got on all fours to suck in the sea air. He felt relieved. When he heard a growl, he looked up and saw he had another problem.

A man in a white towelling dressing gown was leaning over the rails just a few yards away. It wasn't just anyone being sick over the side either. It was Wacko Jacko.

Jacko had probably been on the way to the dining room for a greasy breakfast when he suddenly felt the urge to purge.

There was more than seasickness going on though. The sea was millpond-calm and the sky was endlessly blue and cloudless, but it sounded like Jacko was putting together the backing vocals for *Message in a Beer Bottle*.

Ahead William could see Benny and Luigi disappearing through a door along the deck.

He'd be dead meat if Jacko turned around. What he saw in his mind's eye was his corpse floating in the water below with vomit and regurgitated beer.

He had to get across to the other side of the deck, but how would he get past Jacko without risking detection?

Think, think, think. He closed his eyes.

When he opened them the first thing he saw was a metal staircase to his right. That was it! Those steps would surely lead him to the other side of the deck, and he was bound to find another entrance to the dining room from there.

So he got to his feet and dashed towards it, the cage swinging from his left hand.

He started taking the steps two at a time, trying to put space between him and Jacko as quickly as he could.

But a sharp pain in his upper left leg caused him to stop halfway up, and grab the back of his thigh. When he turned around, he saw Wacko Jacko was now stretching back on the rails behind him. The grizzled man was wiping his mouth with a hand. He might well have been looking at the seagulls sitting on the navigational mast at first but the breadth of his vision widened, then seemed to focus on the staircase.

Suddenly, Wacko Jacko catapulted himself off the rails towards the bottom of the steps with a war cry, a flurry of white towelling, a flash of pink and a clump of pubic hair.

William turned and hobbled upwards as fast as his legs would go.

Goodness knows what the bathers at the top thought when a hobbling man carrying a cage started hopscotching over them? Who knew the ship's swimming pool would be up here? This made it harder to get to the other side. The only way to do that was to weave through all the bodies in their colourful array of bathing suits who were out in great numbers enjoying the morning, winter sun.

When people started to scream, William chanced another look behind him.

A naked man trailing a white towelling cape was in hot pursuit.

But closing in on him were the ship's new security men, Kareem and Wilt, aka Benny and Luigi.

It they saw William, they didn't show it. William suspected they were too intent on crash-tackling the streaker. The cry and the almighty splash behind him told him they had got their man!

———

Christopher had taken Auntie Eloise to breakfast to celebrate the deal they had just sealed with a handshake in her lounge.

She giggled. 'William will be mystified.'

'It'll serve him right.' Captain Rose smirked. 'No-one tries to whack things over me and gets away with it.'

'But what if he finds his rabbits? He might reconsider making me disappear?'

Captain Rose laughed. 'This is a big ship. They might be anywhere.'

'But what if?'

'Oh auntie, you worry too much. All you need to focus on is the insurance payout you'll be getting. Do you really think I'd let this so-called magician diddle me out of my 50 per cent?'

The Maître d' had seated them at Captain Rose's favourite table by the window, which was close to the dumbwaiter that came up from the kitchen with piping hot food.

Captain Rose saw Bob the waiter crossing the room. He wasn't acquainted with all the crew but Bob brought back painful memories. How could he forget the commotion Bob had caused when that lady had brought her poodle into the dining room?

Some stupid person in the booking office had fallen for her bogus story that she was blind and needed to bring her guide dog on the ship.

It turned out to be not a golden labrador but a little white poodle named Rocky. Who even calls a dog Rocky unless it's one of those American fighting dogs!

All cruise long, Mrs Brown had kept up her pretence. She had dark glasses and a white cane, and Rocky towed her everywhere on a lead.

But all hell broke loose the first time he led her into the dining room.

Bob had leapt up on to one of the tables, which had caused a chain reaction of panic. Some passengers tried to hide under tables, others had bolted for the exits. No-one really knew what was going on.

Bob spent the rest of the voyage in sick bay. He claimed to be highly allergic to animals, which was the only reason he said he had come to work on a cruise ship. It served himself right for his pay being docked! He was lucky Captain Rose didn't wring his neck!

Captain Rose snapped out of his unpleasant recollection when a dripping wet man came through the door on the other side of the dining room.

Kareem looked around, then started walking across the packed room, leaving wet footprints all the way, coming to a halt by his table.

'Sorry to disturb you, boss.'

'You're all wet!' Captain Rose glared at him.

'That's because we apprehended a streaker up at the swimming pool. Well, *in* the pool.'

'A streaker?'

The security man nodded, spraying droplets of water towards the table. 'He was as naked as a j-bird and stinking of too much beer. What do you want us to do with him?'

Captain Rose scratched his head, and looked towards a window, thinking. 'I guess we have no choice but to use the cell down on D Deck, near the kitchens,' he said when he had returned his gaze to Kareem. He sighed. 'You'll have to relocate what's in there but then you better lock him up. We can offload him to the police when we reach Cairns.'

———

Captain Rose looked up in time to see Bob walk over to the dumbwaiter.

Bob peered through the glass with the look of someone who

thought the light was playing tricks with his eyes. It was only when he slid open the door, he actually screamed.

It was like slow motion.

Out hopped four startled rabbits that went in four directions under the tables.

The dining room erupted into screams. Some people leapt up on chairs, others escaped through the nearest exits.

Kareem just stood there dripping. 'Is this ship always this crazy, boss?'

————

This definitely was not going to plan.

First, the Hawaiian shirt had flashed past him like a fire engine.

Now William was standing at the door, clutching the empty cage with one hand and his left hamstring in the other, and trying to comprehend the chaos unfolding before his eyes.

He was so gobsmacked, he didn't know he was blocking the escape path until he realised people were making a beeline for the door on the other side of the room.

He could see Captain Rose and Miss Jones by the window on the other side. He could also see the back of a large man he knew was Benny.

————

When Benny turned and started heading back his way, William ducked behind the door.

Benny turned left and went back the way he came.

William was happy to see the back of him rapidly getting smaller.

He looked around the deck, searching for a place to stash the cage, now he obviously wouldn't be needing it.

His eyes fell on a lifeboat suspended above the deck, which would make an excellent hiding place if only he could reach it. He decided in an instant he couldn't. So he just left the cage on a deck chair, and he limped back towards the pool.

He had no idea what had become of Wacko Jacko. For all he knew, Benny had been seeking advice from the captain on what to do with his sodden corpse.

So up the stairs he went again. He winced every second rung.

He was comforted when he saw there weren't swirls of blood in the pool and the sunbathers had returned to their tranquility.

He hopscotched awkwardly over the bodies and towels again and when he got to the other side, he looked down and saw Benny and Luigi were frogmarching Wacko Jacko along the lower deck.

Benny was wrestling his prisoner forward. Luigi was running alongside, holding his cap over Wacko Jacko's naughty bits.

William guessed where they were taking him.

William scampered down the staircase, using the rails for support.

As he had suspected, they disappeared into the staff corridor.

He hobbled down the first flight of stairs, and hovered on the landing waiting for their voices to disappear down below.

He heard a door open, then Luigi's voice.

'I'll just get the basketball from the room. I hear there's a ring down there.'

'Well, just get a move on.' Benny sounded as agitated as Luigi sounded excited.

William heard the door close and everything went quiet.

William waited a good minute before descending again.

It was only when he reached the bottom, he realised he should have waited longer.

He could see them at the other end of the corridor near the ladder.

William flattened himself against a door and thought: this will be interesting.

But it was an anti-climax.

He heard a scream that told him someone had just pushed Wacko Jacko into the void.

This reconfirmed to William something he had already guessed. These weren't the kinds of ruthless men to let slip your guard.

'Did you really have to do that?' he heard Luigi say.

'Did you have any better ideas of how to get him down there?'

'You didn't even give me a chance to come up with a plan.'

'You ever come through with a plan yet?'

'You could have killed him! How would we have explained that to the captain?'

'How come I can hear him moaning then. He obviously ain't dead.'

William heard the ball bouncing at the bottom, and then he heard the thugs as they climbed down the ladder.

Benny shouted: 'Did you just pass gas again?'

'No.' Luigi sounded indignant. 'Why do you keep saying that?'

'Well, you're always eating that Toscano kale … oh, that's goddamn awful!'

William leant back against the door. What to do now?

This thought was taken away from him by gravity as the door was opened inwards. William was lucky not to bang his head on the corner of a bunk as he landed on his back. He saw Joe looking down at him.

'Sorry. I didn't know you were there,' the barman said. 'Are you all right?'

'I think so.' William turned himself around and got up to his knees, then put a hand on the end of the bunk to leverage himself on to his feet. His left thigh hurt.

Joe looked relieved. 'I thought you must have done a runner.'

'I'm on a ship! Where would I run to?'

'No idea.' Joe shrugged. 'But you weren't in your bunk when I came in early this morning, and when I woke up just now all your gear was gone.'

'You see or hear Pedro come and collect my things.'

'Did he? When?'

'A good hour ago.'

Joe smiled. 'I sleep like the dead, man. I'm not sure why I even woke up just now. This is like the middle of the night for me.' Then he frowned. 'So where did you go?'

This was the opening William needed. 'Can you keep a secret?'

Joe just looked at him. 'I'm a barman. I keep secrets for a living.'

'Well, I suppose I can tell you. The captain has re-tasked me.'

'You're not a magician any more?'

'Haven't you heard about multi-skilling?'

Joe looked at him blankly.

'It's a word you'll be hearing a lot of in the future.'

Joe broke into a smile. 'I get it now. You're like Dr Who. You've come from the future to warn me.'

'Believe me, if I had been in the future I would have stayed in the future where I am sure it's a lot safer than this ship.'

'So what's your real reason for sneaking around?'

'I told you. Captain Rose has re-tasked me. He's given me the authority to deputise whoever I need to help me.'

'Like cowboys? A posse, you mean?'

'Very similar. I can't tell you everything until you need to know it.' He grabbed the back of his sore thigh. 'What I can tell you is I need your help.'

SEVEN
BASKETBALL BLUES

AS HE CLIMBED DOWN, William could hear Joe's boots clunking on the rungs near his head.

William stopped and looked up. 'I told you that you had to be quiet,' he hissed. 'Like a ninja.'

Joe looked down beneath his left armpit. 'A what?'

'Never mind,' William whispered upwards. 'That's another word you'll hear a lot of in the future.'

When they both got to the bottom, the smell of cabbage enveloped them. Joe scowled at him. 'How *do* you know so much about the future?'

'Call it intuition.' William scratched his head. 'I like to look ahead a lot. We really do have to be quiet though.'

William poked a thumb in the direction of the jail. 'Hear that?'

'It sounds like a basketball being bounced,' Joe said. 'Is this what all this is about? You need another player? Sheesh, man! You'll just be a liability with that sore leg.'

'Keep your voice down, will you?' William waved his hands downwards. 'I have no intention of playing that stupid Yanky game, with or without my injury. I need your strength to help me close the heavy door.'

'You what?'

William pointed to the nearby pool of blood on the rubber matting, though it looked more like water in this yellowy light. 'I told you: I'm on a mission from the captain. Those new security men are gangsters and we need to contain them down here before they endanger the ship.'

'Yeah right!'

William shook his head. 'You're not taking this seriously! Keep your head down. It's quite likely these fellows have guns.' He turned. 'Follow me.'

They were at the door in a jiffy.

Luigi was shooting hoops at the other end of the room.

Benny was lying on a bench in the corner of the room lifting weights.

They crouched down. William pointed to the jail cell where a man was lying on the floor moaning among the potato sacks. 'See what they've done,' he said softly. 'You don't want to mess with these ruffians.'

Joe looked at him with a new-found look of seriousness. 'Should we try to rescue him?' he whispered.

'Goodness, no. He's one of the baddies, too. I need you to help me close this heavy door.' He glanced at the side of the airlock.

'You sure the captain is OK with this? We've done drills. Once closed, this door can't be opened while we're at sea.'

'Sure I'm sure.' He said that a little too loudly, because it made Benny look up. If looks could kill, William would be dead.

Next thing, there came a thump from the weights being thrown aside, and Benny was bolting up the room shouting.

'Quick.' William reached around the corner for the handle.

Benny was nearly upon them when Joe helped him drag the door shut. It locked into place with a satisfying click.

———

William spent most of the rest of the day lying low in Miss Jones's cabin.

'If your nephew comes to the door, tell him you haven't seen me,' he told her from the comfort of the sofa where he was literally lying low in the hope of catching up on sleep and resting his sore leg.

'Oh, like he'll fall for that!'

'Why wouldn't he?' He raised his head.

'He already knows you're hiding here. Not that it really matters. He knows he'll see you tonight.'

'Tonight?' William shouldn't have sprung to his feet. Ouch!

'The magic show, remember? In the cabaret room after dinner?'

'You can't expect me to go through with that now? You saw them? My rabbits have scarpered and I strained my hammy trying to round them up.'

Miss Jones held up her leotards in her left hand. 'Looks like we're back to Plan B again. I've taken the liberty of asking the crew to set up the prop we talked about.'

In her right hand she held a folded-up piece of paper she now thrust at William.

He felt puzzled as he took it. 'What's this?'

'It's my last will and testament. We'll need to get Christopher to witness it at dinner tonight.'

He unfolded it and examined it. The will bequeathed her assets to Captain Rose. Everything!

He couldn't believe his eyes. 'This is not what we agreed!'

'Relax. We have to get him on board. When I disappear, the last thing we need is for him to pull this ship apart looking for me.'

'What are you saying?' He waved the document. 'That if he knows about this, he won't bother putting much effort into looking for you?'

'That's exactly what I mean. You don't know him as well as I do. He has big gambling debts. He won't be looking for me very hard at all if he knows there's a big cheque riding on me not being found.'

She walked over to the table and dug into her handbag for another piece of paper she handed over.

William looked at it. This document also said it was her last will and testament, but it was dated one day later than the previous one. This one ceded all of the booty to William.

'He'll never agree to this.'

'He doesn't have to. You and him can witness the other one tonight. You can keep the papers for safe-keeping. That way you can practise his signature for as long as you need to so "he" can witness the new one.'

'Eloise! That's forgery.'

She shrugged. 'So? It's not like you've never done it before?'

He bristled. 'When have I ever done that?'

'On your school sick notes.'

He went pale. 'How do you know about that?'

'James told me obviously.'

William continued looking at her quizzically. 'How did he find out?'

'I think he knew the owner of the snooker hall you went to when you wagged school, and he put two and two together.'

'And he told you this? Why?'

'I told you. He promised to marry me. He thought I had a right to know.'

She dug into her pocket and handed over another piece of paper.

He started unfolding it. 'What's this?'

'It's for you to hang on to if they question why I'd give you all my money. It's my signed and dated declaration that you're my step-son, and you're my next of kin.'

EIGHT
SHOWTIME

WILLIAM LIMPED into the cabaret room dressed in his sparkly cape and over-sized top hat, with his magic wand tucked beneath his left arm.

Miss Jones wore a robe, and they walked across the cabaret room towards the captain's table.

Captain Rose, stood, doffed his cap and gave a small bow as they approached the table, which was at the front of the cabaret room close to the performance platform, on which sat a big box covered with red crepe paper.

'I'm going to enjoy this show,' Captain Rose said loud enough for everyone in the vicinity to hear. He was wearing a white uniform, which made the nicotine-yellow fingers on both his hands even more conspicuous.

As he stood there, he whispered to William from the corner of his mouth. 'You'd better not screw this up. I can detect a fake limp from a mile away, and no-one pulls a sickie on my watch.'

Then he pulled out a chair for his auntie. 'I hope the pre-show nerves won't spoil your appetite. I hope you like duck a l'orange with winter vegetables.'

William had to pull back his own chair. 'For your information, I hurt my leg trying to catch *your* rabbits.'

'Don't you mean *your* rabbits. When I get to the bottom of who put them in the dumbwaiter, someone's going to pay big time. You better hope that's not you, mister!'

Captain Rose placed his cap on the table and smiled as he looked around. 'I'm guessing this is a classier crowd than your normal house.'

William couldn't disagree. The tables around him were filling up. The whole area was carpeted in a pattern of light blue anchors on a navy blue background but the murmuring noise level in the room was rising as people introduced themselves to the others at their table and started chatting. Men in suits and ties, women in gowns. The ship's prospectus had promised them a crooner.

William shrugged. 'The thing is Christopher — I can call you Christopher?'

'No, you can't.'

'The thing is: I only brought three rabbits on to this ship. It's obvious the rabbits you saw in the dumbwaiter aren't actually mine.'

'How's it obvious? The only obvious thing, which is so obvious it escaped your attention, is that one of them must have been pregnant.'

'Oh, that's quite impossible.'

'Why, may I ask?'

'They are all boy rabbits.'

'Boys? How could you possibly know that?' William could have sworn he saw flecks of white foam at the corner of the captain's mouth.

'My, you have been at sea too long if you can't tell the difference between boys and girls. But I assure you I can tell, which means this ship obviously has a rabbit problem.'

'What are you implying?'

'I'm not implying anything. Do you do shipboard drills to cope with rabbit plagues?'

————

Captain Rose stamped a hand so hard on the table, his knife did a somersault.

'How dare you claim my ship has some kind of plague? If the ship's jail weren't otherwise occupied, I'd be in my rights to have you thrown in there for trying to spread malicious gossip.'

William smiled. 'You forget I am also a lawyer as well as a student of rabbit genitalia.'

Captain Rose didn't have time to respond before a waiter over his right shoulder laid a plate of food in front of him. The captain stared at the plate then turned to the waiter and hissed. 'What is this?'

'Duck a l'orange, sir.'

'I can see that. But why are there no vegetables on my plate?'

'There are no vegetables on anyone's plate, sir.'

Captain Rose looked around the other tables, which confirmed this.

'I know for a fact that we loaded several bags of brussels sprouts in Hobart,' he fumed. 'The menu promises winter vegetables.' He slammed his fist on the table again and everyone's plates shuddered. 'Which clot decided to leave them off?'

'You did, sir.'

Captain Rose stood up and clenched his fists. 'Me? You insubordinate …'

The waiter held up both palms. 'I thought you must have given the order to have the door closed.'

'What door?'

'The airlock between the kitchen and the pantry. We no longer have access to the vegetables.'

'That's preposterous. I never gave any such order. Can't someone open the door?'

'That would be against regulations at sea, sir.'

Captain Rose slumped back in his chair. 'Those new Americans, blast them! Someone should have told them that door is not allowed to be closed.'

Miss Jones reached out and touched him. 'Are you all right, Christopher?'

'No, I'm not all right.' He threw his head into his hands. 'No wonder I haven't seen them since this morning. They're probably keeping a low profile because they've realised what they've gone and done.'

William sniffed in the aroma of his plate. 'No use crying over spilt milk or absent vegetables. As we say in show business, the meal must go on.'

Captain Rose waggled a finger at him 'Don't think for a minute this gets you off the hook over those rabbits. As soon as those Americans surface, they're getting a new assignment.'

'So you will ask them to track down my rabbits?'

'That's not what I meant, mister.'

William frowned. 'Are you trying to intimidate me? You do know about the rule of law, don't you?'

'When we're at sea, I am the law.' Captain Rose shook his finger again, but stopped when Miss Jones thrust the folded paper his way.

'What's this, auntie?'

'It's my will. You'll need to sign it, and William can witness it, so it's all legal.'

Captain Rose unfurled the paper. He broke into a smile as he read it. Then he dug an engraved gold pen from his shirt pocket, laid the paper down on the table and signed it with a flourish before handing the pen and paper to William to witness. 'Don't think this gets you off the hook either. And you better hope this magic act of yours goes well. If you harm one hair on my auntie's head, those American marines will be the least of your worries. I'll tear you limb from limb myself.'

———

Captain Rose was pleased with his last piece of theatre. Somehow Auntie Eloise had conned the magician into witnessing the will without question. The little twerp probably thought some kind of swindle was in the offing. Little did he know he was the one who was actually going to be burned.

It didn't take long for everyone to eat the main course, which was washed down with wine, then the desserts, which came in two choices, Black Forest Gateau or steamed pudding and custard.

When coffee and tea was being served, William and Miss Jones stood up.

'Break a leg then.' Christopher smiled as William hobbled towards the raised platform, closely followed by his auntie.

William pulled his white gloves from a pocket as the lights out there were dimmed and the spotlight was switched on to him. 'Welcome, ladies and gentlemen. I must apologise to those of you who were expecting me to sing tonight. The crooner listed on the program has fallen ill.'

The bulk of the people in the crowd groaned.

'Yes, sorry about that.' He put his white gloves on. 'But the good news is you are about to be dazzled by some magic tricks you will never forget.'

Moans came from the darkness.

William removed his top hat and bowed.

'I am Bill the Magnificent, and this ...' He beckoned Miss Jones into the spotlight. '... is my lovely assistant, the Eloquent Eloise.'

With that, Eloise removed her robe, revealing the purple sequinned leotard and her many wrinkles.

'She needs to be sprayed with some starch,' someone shouted.

A young woman stood up. 'Two-timer,' she shouted, breaking into tears. 'I still can't believe this is the old hag you've dumped me for! What have you done with my father?'

Captain Rose didn't know what to make of all that, but how dare she call his auntie an old hag. He stood and squinted in the offender's direction.

He was working up to barking at her as soon as she came into focus, but William beat him to the punch.

'It's OK, Rita. If you care to wait outside until after the show, I'll come and talk to you.'

She walked to the back of the room and out the exit.

Captain Rose made eye contact with the magician, wondering what the hell was going on, but William's returned gaze didn't offer any explanation. He just charged on with the show.

'I must offer two more apologies, ladies and gentlemen. Firstly, on behalf of the captain ...' He pointed to Captain Rose. '... who is clearly not steering the ship right now and very clearly enjoying a glass or six of red wine, he is very sorry there were no vegetables on your plate tonight due to unforeseen circumstances.'

The blood shot to his face, as Captain Rose stood to defend

himself. 'The wheel is in the capable hands of First Officer Christian.' He tried to add a little humour. 'Wallace hasn't hit rocks for months now.'

When the silent reaction told him that little joke hadn't gone down so well, he added: 'And we're working on the veggie problem as we speak.'

'Yes, I'm sure you are,' said William.

Captain Rose knew this was a problem that wasn't going to go away. It'd be a week before they finally made landfall in Cairns and that door could be prised open. Sitting down didn't make him feel any better.

'The other apology I have is about the brevity of this magic show,' William said. 'I'm sorry to say that's of the captain's making, too. Long story short, it's his fault I've hurt my leg, which means Eloise and I have had no time to rehearse at all.'

Boos came from the darkness.

William motioned for silence with downward movements of his hands. 'To be fair, it's not all his fault. I mean, he wasn't to know the crooner would pull out sick. But just as the captain *is the law* at sea, the buck stops at him when things go wrong.'

More boos, and William did the downward hands thing again.

'This means, ladies and gentlemen, we only have one trick to show you tonight.'

Captain Rose tried to ignore the angry gazes he felt burning into the back of his head.

When the new round of boos had subsided, William found voice again.

'I can reveal though this one trick is a trick to end all tricks. I think you are going to be impressed.'

He paused for effect, then pointed to the coffin-shaped red box lying on the floor behind him.

'If you please, I am going to make my lovely assistant disappear before your very eyes. Eloise? Climb into the box please.'

She did. She had to do it slowly, with her arthritic knees and all but it only took a few minutes.

William closed the flap on the red box, spun it around three times, tapped the top three times, uttered some magic words, and opened the box, which he rotated so the audience could see.

Sure enough, she was gone.

William waved his wand into the four corners of the box to show there were no trick mirrors.

'I know what you're thinking. Amazing, right? You're thinking: where could she have possibly gone? Well, I can't reveal that secret but I can promise you this. After your complementary glasses of port and sherry, I'll make her reappear ...' He tapped his wand on the top of the box three times. 'Right. Back. Here.'

————

William had a smug look on his face when he sat back down.

'I told you I could make her disappear!'

For the benefit of onlookers, Captain Rose tried to make himself look angry. 'She's the only family I have left. Where's she gone?'

William tapped his nose. 'A magician doesn't reveal his tricks. All you need to know is I plan to make Eloise reappear after drinks.'

'You'd better.' Captain Rose lowered his voice to an agitated whisper. 'What do you think you were doing hanging me out to dry in front of all these people? They need to respect the captain so they know they can depend on him in a crisis.'

'Because a good captain always goes down with the ship?'

'Not always. Haven't you heard of delegation? I'm sure First Officer Christian would love to step in. He's not good for much else!'

'How are you going to relieve him at the wheel if you're three-parts full?'

'You'd try to drown your sorrows, too, if you missed your vegetables as much as I miss my vegetables. I still can't believe Benny and Wilt closed that door.'

William stiffened. 'What did you call them? You *do* know their real names?'

Captain Rose held his glass up and examined the remaining dregs. 'This stuff must be making me slur my words. It is noisy in here, too.'

He drained his drink, then turned around so he could summon the nearest waiter with a port bottle.

He lit a cigarette, all the time watching his glass being refilled.

Then he stretched back and put his hands behind his head, cigarette bobbing in his mouth.

William frowned. 'Are you absolutely certain you don't have to be careful how much you drink?'

Captain Rose removed the cigarette from his mouth and blew out a stream of smoke. 'Like they breath-test a lot of cruise-liner captains! The only time I need to be sober is when I'm near things we can bump into, like coming into port.'

He laughed into the air. 'You, on the other hand, are under the microscope every single night you do your show. STARTING TONIGHT.'

He drained his glass, banged it down, then he reached over and grabbed the glass in front of where his auntie had been sitting. 'I have a feeling Auntie Eloise won't be needing this. Waste not, want not.'

———

William was quite sure Captain Rose had called the Americans by their real names. He'd have to nut out what was going on when he had more time. Right now, he was limping across the platform to the red box, theatrically holding up his wand.

He turned around and doffed his hat again.

'Ladies and gentlemen, I am about to do the impossible. You witnessed the disappearance of the lovely Eloise.' He opened the side of the box again and tilted it so they could see it was still empty. He waved his wand round again.

'I need a volunteer to come and inspect the box.'

A flurry of hands went up and he surveyed the room.

'You,' he said, and a small girl in a green dress approached the stage.

'What's your name, sweetie?' She only came up to his armpits and when she smiled, she was missing one top tooth.

'Lisa.'

'Hello, Lisa. I'm guessing you're, let me see …' He looked her over '… aged about 21.'

'Seven' she corrected him, and the crowd laughed, even Captain Rose.

'Seven!' William feigned shock. 'A lot of people are relying on you to verify that this box is empty. Can you do that?'

Lisa nodded, and he led her over to the red box.

'Now I want you to be honest. What can you see in there?'

'Hmmm, dust.'

'Dust? I shall speak to the man who's in charge of the cleaners.' He looked down to the captain, who scowled back.

William turned his attention back to the little girl, who was now waving a hand around the inside of the box. 'Say, you don't think my assistant has turned into dust?'

She flashed a tooth-deficient smile again. 'I dunno. She was pretty old!'

'Pretty old! Are you going to say that to her face when I make her reappear?'

Lisa shrugged. 'I don't think she's coming back.'

William looked down at her. 'Oh you don't? Why do you say that?'

She shrugged again. 'Well, she's not here — that's for sure.'

William squeezed her shoulder. 'You heard the kid, ladies and gentlemen. Eloise is no where to be seen.' He bent down. 'You go back to your parents now, Lisa. Thank you for your help.'

He rose to his full height and started clapping. 'Put your hands together, ladies and gentlemen, for my new young assistant … Lisa.'

He stood there until the clapping had stopped.

'And now,' he announced, 'I need someone to do a drumroll on the table.'

At least three people obliged. Shame they didn't synchronise.

'You'll be able to tell your grandchildren you once saw Bill the Magnificent do the impossible even though he was only on one leg. It is one thing to make a person disappear but only the truly great magicians can make the disappeared reappear.'

He closed the lid, and turned the box on its side so it would now open to the full view of the audience.

'Are you ready to witness the remarkable?'

'Yes,' came the reply.

He cocked his ear. 'I didn't hear you!'

'Yes,' they chanted more loudly.

'I'm so glad you are with me. But I need one more thing. When I tap this box three times with my magic wand, I need you all to say: COME BACK, ELOISE.'

This is what happened.

He tapped the box three times, and led the chant: 'COME BACK, ELOISE.'

When William pulled back the lid, even he was surprised.

He obviously didn't really expect to see Miss Jones. But he certainly didn't expect to see a black and white rabbit in there.

———

This was yet another rabbit that wasn't one of his rabbits or one of the rabbits he had loaded into the dumbwaiter. He knew this because the four rabbits he had found in the jail were all white rabbits, as were the three he had brought aboard.

The rabbit that wrinkled its nose as it looked up at him was more black than white. Before William could react, the rabbit jumped out of the box and disappeared under the captain's table.

No-one in the room jumped. Most of them, Captain Rose excepted, were roaring with laughter. They obviously thought it was all part of the act.

William tried to keep his composure. 'I'll try that again, shall I?'

He closed the lid and led another chant. 'COME BACK, ELOISE.'

He opened the lid.

This time a tan-coloured rabbit hopped out of the box and scurried into the crowd.

William straightened his hat and swished his cape.

'Sorry. I'll try again.'

He closed the lid again, and asked the audience to shout at the top of their voices 'COME BACK, ELOISE.'

As he began opening the lid, he wondered what coloured rabbit he'd find this time.

But he needn't have worried.

The box was empty, aside from the dust Lisa had already identified. Oh, and some rabbit poop that he was sure hadn't been there before.

Captain Rose stood up before William could explain.

He stubbed out his cigarette in the ashtray like he was squashing a bug, then pointed his finger at William. 'I knew it! What have you done with my auntie?'

William said the first thing that came into his head. 'I don't know how I did it, but I seem to have turned her into a rabbit. Perhaps two rabbits.'

'She must be here somewhere. I'll have the whole ship searched.'

William turned his attention to the audience. 'I am truly sorry, ladies and gentlemen. As I said, if the captain here had given us even just a little time to rehearse ...'

Captain Rose was outraged. 'You have the audacity to blame me for your incompetence!'

'Maybe if I have another go tomorrow night, I can bring her back?'

Captain Rose waggled his finger. 'Oh no. You don't get out of it this easily. You're sacked! And mark my words, I'd have you thrown in the ship's jail if it was still accessible.'

NINE
LOOKING OUT FOR RUBBER DUCKS

RITA WAS STANDING outside the door when William finally left the room pretending to look bewildered and humiliated, and limping more than he really needed to. He held Eloise's last will and testament in his hand, with the signature he needed to learn how to forge.

Rita looked at him quizzically. 'I thought you said you had lost your rabbits?'

He nodded, trying to look numb.

'How come two rabbits came out the door earlier then?' He opened his mouth to explain but she got in first. 'Then a whole lot of people rushed out, including that captain who didn't look happy.'

William exhaled like it were the last dregs of air in a balloon. 'He's angry because I made his auntie disappear into thin air, but for some reason I couldn't make her come back.'

'His auntie?'

'The old biddy wearing the sparkly leotards.'

She looked at him blankly.

'Hello? My new assistant! Eloise?'

'Oh her? You made her really disappear? Wow.' Then she began sobbing. 'So did you make my father vanish, too?'

'Certainly not!' William feigned surprise again. 'The last I heard of him was his snoring. Did you by any chance see him go outside looking for a place to throw up? He might have fallen over the side.'

She looked daggers at him. 'How could you say such a thing!' Her eyes were watery. 'On my birthday too?'

'Oh, I wouldn't worry.' William put an arm around her. 'It wouldn't be the first time your dad has gone into hiding. He's probably growing a beard and carving a false nose as we speak. That's what you do when you're on the run.'

'You really think so?' She wiped away tears with the back of her hands.

'I know so. Take it from a lawyer who has lots of experience in that area.' He really did feel sorry for her at that moment. The hormones yo-yo-ing through a teenager's body were tough enough, throw in the pregnancy hormones, and a missing father, and you had a hormonal bungee jump going on.

So he wasn't surprised when she broke into a smile again. 'How come you never let me in on that new act?'

'What new act?'

'Making your assistant disappear.'

William's eyes narrowed. 'I told you to go away. Isn't that near enough?'

'But you couldn't make her reappear?' She started laughing.

He gave her a dark look. 'You think it's funny I now have no idea where Miss Jones is?'

This wasn't exactly true. He knew she'd be hiding under the bed in her cabin. Captain Rose for all his bluster wouldn't really be looking too hard for her, thinking he was going to benefit from a huge double-cross. Come the inevitable inquiry, he'd have the perfect excuse for not giving the search his all. He couldn't know it yet his new security men were locked up with his beloved brussels sprouts, but he'd soon find out they were missing, and then he'd be more short-staffed than ever.

Even now, it was hard for William not to think of the big pay-day coming his way. How good would it be to wipe the smile off the smarmy captain's face!

Rita broke William's musings. 'So you'll be looking for a new assistant?'

'What?' It took him a moment to process her hopeful tone. 'Certainly not! I'm devoting all my energies to finding the old one.'

'But what if you can't? What if she's disappeared forever?'

Think, think, think. William tried to work out what to say. 'Er, you're starting to show, Rita. I can't take you on stage like that. Maybe it'll become acceptable in the future. You know my views: I certainly hope so. But not now, not in 1974.'

'It's still only a little bump.'

'Well, it's academic anyway. The captain has sacked me. He's reassigned me to other duties.'

'What kind of duties?'

'I hate to think. Scrubbing the deck? Walking the plank? At least I know I won't be peeling potatoes.'

'How do you know that?'

'Let's not go there, shall we?'

He turned to leave but stopped and grabbed her hand, which he squeezed. 'Look, I'm sure your father will turn up somewhere.' He suppressed the urge to say: maybe on a "wanted" poster. 'But you'll have to excuse me. Did I tell you how I injured my leg?' He didn't wait for an answer. 'Another time, OK? I'm so mentally drained, I need to get back to my cabin and try to think why this all went wrong.'

———

William looked under the bed, and scratched his head 'Eloise, where are you?'

There was no answer.

He walked back into the main room and opened the broom cupboard door.

Nothing presented itself other than stink and brooms.

A knock came at the door, which made his heart skip a beat. He stood still until he heard a key turning the lock.

Now his heart was racing, and so was his mind.

It couldn't be her. Why would she knock?

Then the door swung open and it became clear.

'I thought I'd find you here!' Captain Rose made no attempt to remove his hat as he stepped inside. He acted much more sober now. 'The thing is: is Auntie Eloise here, too?'

William put his hands on his hips. 'You never cease to amaze me! You saw her vanish. Why would she be here?'

'You don't expect me to believe that mumbo jumbo. She has to be somewhere.'

William scratched his scalp. 'How did you even get the key to this cabin?'

'I'm the captain.' His eyes narrowed. 'I have access to the master-key.'

'That doesn't give you the right to just barge right in here.'

'I have every right — no, duty — when I'm concerned about the safety and welfare of one of my passengers. Normally I'd task the search to my security officers. But I don't know where those Americans are hiding and I'd prefer to devote my time and energy looking for Auntie Eloise rather than search for them.'

'Well, she's not here, as you can see.'

Captain Rose scowled at him. 'You don't mind if I have a look around?'

'If I did, would it stop you?'

'No.' Captain Rose turned towards the bedroom and ensuite, and William followed a few steps behind. Captain Rose started opening cupboards and slamming them. He knelt down to look under the bed, lingering until his eyes had adjusted to the light. He pulled out every coat-hangared garment from the wardrobe and threw them on the bed until there was no more place potentially to hide.

'Satisfied?' William pouted.

'Not until I check the other room.'

William followed him back into the sitting room.

Captain Rose pointed to the broom cupboard. 'Why didn't I look in there first? That's tall enough for her to stand up in?'

'Nothing in there but brooms. I already checked.'

'As if I'm going to believe you!' Captain Rose pulled on the handle but stepped back as soon as he opened it and a rabbit hopped past him and into the bedroom. He stared at William, waiting for an explanation.

'I've never seen that rabbit before in my life.' William stared at the space where the rabbit had been, and his eyes panned to the bedroom door. 'When are you going to accept you have a rabbit problem on this ship?'

'You were the one who introduced rabbits on to this liner.'

'Three white, *male* rabbits. I can't be held responsible for what's becoming a plague.'

'Three *magic* rabbits.'

'I thought you didn't believe in *mumbo jumbo*?'

'Well, something's going on.' He stepped towards William and eyeballed him. 'If I find out you've had anything to do with the disappearance of the Yanks—'

'Benny and Luigi?'

'Who?'

'That's what you called them earlier.'

Captain Rose glared down at him. 'You must have misheard me.' William felt a series of small finger stabs on his chest as the captain emphasised his point. 'Their names are Kareem and Wilt. Get it, mister.'

'You can't lay your hands on a passenger!'

'You're not a passenger. You're staff.'

'You sacked me.'

'Only from that position. I redeployed you, remember?'

'Good luck with that. The only two skills I have involve the law and magic, and I've injured my leg.'

'You have two good eyes, don't you? Good eyesight is all you need to be the nightwatchman on a ship. And a warm coat.'

The blood drained from William's face. 'What?'

'That's the job I've redeployed you to. Your new role is to stand on the bow upper deck all night and look out for things that have fallen off freighters.'

'You're kidding?'

Captain Rose smiled like he was enjoying this. 'No, I'm serious. You wouldn't believe the shipping hazards floating around. I've seen half-submerged shipping containers I've had to steer around, and flotillas of yellow plastic ducks I've had to bust up.'

'Oh great! So you want me to keep an eye out for ducks!'

'And rabbits. And if you happen to see Kareem and Wilt sneaking around the deck in the dark, motion to the boys inside the bridge. They'll be able to send someone to wake me.'

———

If only the magician could have seen the look on his little face! Priceless!

'I've never heard of the position of nightwatchman on a ship,' he protested.

'Sure you have,' said Captain Rose. 'In the old days we used to send them up to the crow's nest. Instead of shouting "land ahoy", they now shout "shipping container ahoy".'

'You're making this up. I bet the union would have a bit to say about all this.'

The captain bore through his eyes. 'Are you thick? I told you when I hired you: THIS IS A NO-UNION SHIP.'

'You didn't tell me any such thing. I would have remembered you shouting at me.'

'You sure I didn't I tell you?' The captain lowered his voice and scratched his neck. 'You probably didn't ask.'

'You certainly didn't tell me I could be redeployed from the position of magician.'

'You're a slow learner, aren't you? Didn't I just make myself clear? If you had asked, I would have told you.' He glanced at his watch. 'Not to mention you're a tardy timekeeper.'

'What are you talking about?'

'You were supposed to be at your watching post an hour ago.'

'But you've just told me! And the nearest thing I have to a warm coat is my magician's cape.'

Captain Rose shook his head. 'You'll have to try running on the spot to keep warm then. You'd never forgive yourself if this ship hit a semi-submerged object and sank. You'd be responsible for the loss of all those lives.'

'Yours included. But I'd probably be happy dancing on *your* grave.'

'You forget I know where the best lifeboats are.'

'So you weren't joking about not going down with the ship?'

'I never joke. NOW GET TO YOUR POST, MISTER. THAT'S AN ORDER.'

'No need to shout.' William grabbed his cape from a cloak rack in the corner and headed out the room, slamming the door behind him.

Captain Rose started to whistle as he followed, more relaxed.

He was walking on air as he went along the hall, and up two flights of stairs towards his penthouse cabin.

OK, so not everything was going to plan?

How they were going to spend so many days at sea without vegetables was a problem he really had to address.

And where the hell were Benny and Luigi?

The good thing is he already had their bribe money stashed away in his cabin.

The even better thing is he had an even bigger nest-egg there, too.

He put his key in his lock and opened the door.

As soon as he walked in, he saw her sitting at the kitchen table.

Auntie Eloise lifted her head. 'Is it all going to plan, Christopher?'

TEN
ONE MORE THING, SAILOR

WILLIAM WAS SHAKEN AWAKE.

He opened his eyes and saw Captain Rose looking down on him. Then he realised the captain's hand was on his shoulder.

'What the hell are you doing here?'

Captain Rose looked furious. 'What are you doing sleeping in Auntie Eloise's bed?'

William dragged himself up on his pillows and rubbed his eyes. 'I'm not exactly sleeping now, am I?' He looked around for a clock. 'What time is it?'

'Seven o'clock. I have something else for you to do.'

'Seven! I only got off my shift at six. Surely I'm allowed more than an hour's break?'

'This is a non-union ship, remember?'

'What's so urgent?' William rubbed his eyes again. 'If I have to stay awake in the cold all night again I need my sleep.'

'Don't you understand? I'm re-tasking you.'

'Re-tasking me? I was just getting the hang of the last task.'

Captain Rose smoothed down one of his navy blue sleeves. 'The boys on the bridge tell me you didn't spot a single shipping container.'

'What's with the blue uniform? I could have sworn you were dressed in white last night.'

Captain Rose looked skywards. 'You've got a lot to learn, mister. That was my formal uniform I wear to dinner. This is what I wear during the day.'

'That so? You ever get mixed up? Blue socks, white shorts, blue shirt, white hat. You could be a mascot for North Melbourne.'

Captain Rose looked daggers at him. 'You do know we still do burials at sea?'

'Are you threatening me?'

'You still haven't explained why you didn't spot any errant containers overnight.'

'I thought that'd be obvious. BECAUSE THERE WERE NONE. NOR ICEBERGS. I DIDN'T SEE ANY RUBBER DUCKS EITHER.'

'I've only got your word for that.'

'We didn't sink in the middle of the night, did we?'

Captain Rose smiled. 'That gives me some confidence for your new task then.'

William threw back the covers, and threw his legs towards the floor. He had forgotten he had a sore leg but the sudden pain reminded him.

He yelled.

Captain Rose showed not an ounce of sympathy. 'There's no room for malingerers on this ship.'

William sat on the side of the bed and yawned. 'So what do you want me to do now?'

The captain straightened his cap. 'I was awake half the night trying to figure it out. We need to find us some more vegetables.'

'You can't work out how to open that door, eh?' William looked up at him. 'Too bad.'

The captain gave William another blast of his rancid breath. 'The good news is we're now anchored not far from a little island, which has a sizeable building, which gives me hope it might just have a sizeable veggie patch, too.'

William sensed what was coming. 'What's the bad news?'

'Bad news?' The captain smiled. 'Who mentioned bad news? I thought you'd appreciate a spot of fresh air?'

'I got plenty of that last night, thanks.'

'But this time you'll be manning the oars of a small dinghy with your nose right to the wind.'

'A dinghy? Me? With my sore leg? How many others will be rowing?'

'Just you. There's only room for two in the dinghy, but don't worry, I'll be the other one. You have to have a coxswain.'

'I've never rowed a boat in my life!'

The captain smiled again. 'Lucky you have two healthy arms then.'

'You're enjoying this, aren't you?' William stood up and scratched his belly. 'We can put a man on the moon but you're telling me you haven't got some small vessel with an outboard motor.'

'We have to be careful not to damage the delicate ecology of shore-lines by polluting them with marine diesel or bombarding them with powerful little waves.'

'You're kidding me, aren't you? You never struck me as a new-age sensitive guy? You don't think I'd be better use staying here and continuing my search for Eloise?'

'When I arrived here, you didn't look to me like you were doing much searching.'

'Which reminds me, have you ever heard of knocking?'

'Why aren't you sleeping in the quarters this cruise company has assigned you as a member of this crew?'

'Fair suck of the sav! I only came back here this morning to check if she had turned up. When I saw her bed hadn't been slept in, I, well …'

'You know where she is, don't you? You know she's not coming back?'

'That's not true. As soon as I get some sleep, and can address it with a clear mind, I'm going to try to figure out what I did wrong. If I can retrace my steps, I'm sure I can bring her back.'

'Don't waste your time, mister. I've now got Kareem and Wilt on the job. If anyone can find her, they will.'

'The Americans? Really?' This was the moment William smelt a rat. 'Where did you find them?'

'They found me. They're very remorseful about locking the door when they left the prisoner.'

'Oh, I bet they are! Why don't you get one of them to row you to the island? Big, strong blokes like them? You'd get there quicker than with me.'

'Hmmm, good point.' The captain gazed into the middle distance, as if he were weighing the idea up. 'But no. We really need to go now to catch the tide. They're probably searching on the far reaches of the ship.'

'Now? You mean this very minute? Can't I at least have a cuppa?'

'No time for that. I'll meet you on the lower portside deck in five minutes.' He turned to leave. 'Mind you don't trip over a rabbit. You have no idea how many I saw on the deck on the way over here!'

———

Captain Rose was right. The deck was awash with rabbits.

Even with a gammy left leg, stepping over them wasn't William's biggest problem though. His biggest problem was working out which deck was the portside deck. Since he couldn't see any dock on either side of the ship, William figured portside wasn't what he thought it meant.

He eventually found Captain Rose midway along the left-hand deck, next to four muscular crewmen.

It was another clear day but the water looked grey and the waves were choppy.

He could see the island in the background as he approached.

Captain Rose frowned when William limped towards him. 'Where have you been?' he barked. 'And why are you wearing that top hat?' He frowned even more when he saw William was wearing his sparkly cape and carrying his wand, too. 'We do have oars for you to row the boat.'

'I want to make it absolutely clear to onlookers I'm the ship's magician.' He took his white gloves out of his coat pocket, and put them both on. 'I fully intend to pursue your maniacal behaviour in the courts, and I want lots of witnesses who can testify what you made me do against my wishes.'

Someone approached the captain from behind and tapped him on the shoulder.

As soon as Captain Rose turned around and spoke, he sounded annoyed.

'I should have known it'd be you again, Colonel Billycock-Smythe. Haven't you got anything else to do, you silly old goat?'

The passenger was a tall, elderly Briton with a huge handlebar moustache and a walking stick with an ivory handle. 'I want to know, captain, what you're going to do about all these rabbits?' he said. 'First I get on this ship and find my first-class suite has been double-booked, next I find I've been relegated to a four-berth cabin with damn hard bunks and people I don't care for, now I can't even have a decent game of deck quoits. Don't think I won't be complaining about this rabbit thing, too!'

'Can't you see I'm busy?' Captain Rose pointed to the island. 'I can only solve one problem at a time. You want to eat for the rest of the voyage, don't you?'

William watched as Colonel Billycock-Smythe hobbled off down the deck, muttering.

Captain Rose turned his attention to William. 'See what trouble you've caused?'

'Me! You gave Miss Jones his room didn't you?'

'I'm the captain!'

'And how will that go for you when he complains to the company?'

'If it comes to that, I'll just delegate the blame to an underling. It works every time.'

'You're not entertaining the idea of giving him back Miss Jones's suite?'

'Certainly not! I've seen chaps like him before. He's only on this cruise because it's cheaper than being in a nursing home. With three other people in his cabin, if he croaks before the end of the cruise we'll find out in time to bung his body in the cool room. Do you know how long it takes to fumigate one of the suites if he lies there undiscovered for some days?'

William ran a hand across his forehead. 'For a moment I thought you were going to throw me out.'

'Oh, I am.' Captain Rose's eyes narrowed. 'When we return from the island, you need to haul your sorry backside back to below deck.'

William sighed. 'Aren't you worried about lawsuits?'

Captain Rose frowned. 'Law suits? Is that a new fashion craze?'

'You know exactly what I mean. I'm surprised no-one's gone deaf already from the noise of the engines. And you must know most of your employees smoke in that cabin. It really is unbearable, not a healthy environment at all.'

'Open a window.' Captain Rose broke into a fake smile again. 'Oh, I forgot! You don't have portholes down there.'

William glared. 'Aside from the health of my lungs and my hearing, what if Miss Jones comes back and someone's not there in her suite?'

'You really think I'm a fool, don't you?' Captain Rose winked. 'In any case, there's a wealthy divorcee down on C Deck who'd probably do anything to get an upgrade.'

William shook his head slowly, then gazed towards the island, which was about as big as a soccer field.

He could see coconut trees swaying and a two-storey brick building at one end of the island. 'How far do you think that is away then?'

'Three hundred yards, tops. Mind you, if you had got here half an hour earlier you would have made life easier for yourself. Now the wind has picked up and you'll be rowing against the tide.'

William looked over to the Popeye-like sailors. 'This is your last chance to avoid a law suit by replacing me with someone who's more suited to the task of rowing.'

'Not a chance! I'm not leaving you on this ship where I can't keep an eye on you. Besides, we need those muscle-heads to lower the dinghy. We'll climb down the ladder once the boat is on the water.'

William stepped to the rails and looked over the side. Sure enough, a rope ladder was dangling down to the waterline far, far below.

'Did I tell you I'm afraid of heights?'

'Don't look down then.'

William felt sweaty. 'Do we even know who lives on this island?'

The captain shook his head. 'Nope. It's unchartered. It's not on any of our maps.'

'But you think it might have a veggie patch?'

'You have a better idea?'

William looked around. 'Rabbit soup. Rabbit Pie. Rabbit Stew. Get the idea?'

Captain Rose herded William towards the ladder draped over the side. 'Not going to happen, mister.'

————

William was still wobbling like a jelly when he stepped awkwardly into the dinghy.

He took his place on the bench seat at the back of the little boat and looked up to see Captain Rose still climbing down the ladder. Further up, lots of tiny faces peered over the rail.

William wished it was him still looking down. He felt as tiny as they looked.

When the dinghy began to bob, he saw the big lard was now stepping into the boat and lowering himself to his seat.

When he sat down, Captain Rose released the ropes tethering the dinghy and pushed away from the giant red hull. He nodded towards the oars, which were lying longways inside the boat.

'You're on,' he said.

'But I told you: I've never rowed a boat in my life.'

'It's not rocket science.' Captain Rose rolled his eyes and pointed to the oars. 'See the paddle end? That's the bit that goes in the water.' He pointed alternatively to cradles on either side of the boat. 'They're called rowlocks. You fit the oars into them so they're attached to the dinghy.' He pointed back to the oars. 'See the handles? That's what you hang on to when you're rowing. Point your back to the island, dip your oars in the water simultaneously and drag them back towards you so the boat gets propelled forward.'

'BACKWARDS?' William realised they probably heard him shouting up on the deck. 'I won't be able to see where I'm going!'

'I'll direct you. Just listen to my commands. I might tell you to put more power in the left oar, or into the right oar, or I might say steady as you go. Trust me. I won't let you overshoot the island. And I won't let a Great White sneak up on you.'

'You never told me there were sharks in these waters!'

'I don't know that for sure, but it figures. Sharks roam up and down this coast.'

———

It took them more than an hour to reach the island. Every time they got close, the tide washed them back.

'Can't you put some muscle into it, mister?' the captain barked. Then he cupped his hand so he could light his Viscount.

William knew there was no use protesting. Good thing he had removed his top hat before he started rowing and got out of the shelter of the ship. Otherwise the wind might have blown it into the water, and it'd be lost forever. Little did he know, he'd need that hat many years later.

He turned his head to see how close they were.

'Why have you stopped?' Captain Rose blew smoke out his nose, which made him look a bit like a dragon. The rowboat bobbed and started to turn on the swell.

'Can't you see I'm exhausted? I wanted to see if there were people on the shore waiting for us?'

'Well, there's not — as you can now see. If there were, I would have told you. My guess is they're watching from the windows up there, wondering why there's a ship moored off their island and two people coming ashore.'

The boat had nearly turned right around now. William could feel spray whipping his face but he now had a good view of the house.

He could have sworn he saw flecks of white foam at the edge of Captain Rose's mouth. Then he realised he had been splashed with water, too, which had left him with a soggy, smokeless cigarette drooping from his mouth. 'Here, give me those oars,' he said gruffly. 'Otherwise, we'll never get there.'

When the dinghy hit the sandy beach, William realised too late the captain could step on to hard sand whereas William had to remove his shoes and socks, and roll up his trousers, a movement that caused him more pain. He didn't mind the icy water and feeling the sand on his feet so much, it was the fact the captain found it all so funny.

'You knew, didn't you? That's why you rowed that last bit to shore?'

Captain Rose used his knuckles to wipe the tears of mirth from his eyes. 'You are such a wimp. You'll dry out.'

ELEVEN

RETRACING THE VOYAGE OF CAPTAIN BLIGH

THEY LOOKED up at the house. Ragged curtains flapped gently in the wind behind broken windows, but there was no sign anyone was looking through them.

'Where do you think everyone is?' William said.

Captain Rose shrugged. Just then, the sound of starting engines reached them.

Captain Rose turned. 'What do they think they're doing?' He looked like he was about to scream. Then he did scream, as he took off back to the rowboat on the beach. 'Noooooooooo.'

It was too late though. William could hear the crunch and grind of the anchor being pulled up. By the time Captain Rose had pushed the dinghy back into the water and frantically paddled 50 yards, the big red ship was on the move. What was he thinking? That he could actually catch it? By the time he got 50 more yards, the cruise liner was getting smaller and smaller as it steamed towards the horizon.

Captain Rose stopped splashing.

William stood on the shore, just as perplexed.

Why would they leave them stranded on this island? He turned and looked at the house again. What was this place? Up close, it looked very much derelict — long past habitation. Was that why no-one had responded to the captain's screams?

William turned to look at the sea again. The dinghy had turned around and was coming back this way.

Ten minutes later, an ashen-faced Captain Rose was dragging the boat up the beach again.

———

'What happened?' William said, as he tried to lend a hand.

'Isn't it obvious! I knew I couldn't trust Wallace! He's left us here.'

'But it's just a joke? They'll return for us, right?'

'I doubt it. My guess is Auntie Eloise has double-crossed us both. She probably found the $50,000 in my cabin and did some kind of a deal with First Officer Christian.'

'What $50,000? Wait! You know where Miss Jones is?'

'She's been hiding in my cabin, dummy. It was her idea to cut you out of a share of the insurance money.'

'Let me guess? The $50,000 came from Benny and Luigi?'

'Clever little bloke, aren't you? They came looking for you the morning I set up my recruiting table in Hobart. You had just left, so it's a wonder you didn't run into them. I had no intention of hiring you but when I saw how anxious they were to track you down, I said you were already on the ship but it was going to cost them to get on there, too.'

'So you bribed them?'

'It was the easiest money I ever earned. Half an hour later, they were back at the wharf with a suitcase full of money. I hired them on the spot as my new security detail and spent the rest of the day sweating you'd come back. You have no idea how many proper enter-tainers I knocked back.'

'You know that money is most likely counterfeit, don't you? You know they're mobsters?'

'Tell me something I don't know.'

William pretended to doff the hat that was now sitting on the sand. 'Joe and I locked Benny and Luigi in the recreation room.'

Captain Rose's eyes widened. 'You didn't!'

'We did. My suspicions were raised when you accidentally said their names last night. You confirmed those fears earlier when you said you had found them. Only I knew you couldn't have because you said that door was still locked.'

Captain Rose bowed his head and dragged a palm across his forehead. 'No use worrying about it now, I suppose. I just have to figure out how to get my money back.'

'Good luck with that!'

Captain Rose looked towards the big metal door at the top of the stone steps. 'They must have a phone here. I need to alert the authorities someone has stolen my ship.'

'You haven't looked at the door closely, have you? Look again. It isn't even closed properly.'

'What are you saying? This perfectly good building has been abandoned?'

'Have another look. It's not perfectly good. It's decrepit.' William pointed to an overgrown plot near the house, which might well once have been a veggie garden but now just grew weeds. '

Captain Rose bolted towards the four steps, and William hobbled after him. They stopped on the doorstep. William was right. The only thing keeping them from entering was a tangle of spider webs, which Captain Rose swept away with his hands, which he then wiped on his shirt.

'There could still be a phone here, right?' Panic showed on the captain's face.

They found a black phone in a dark room inside. The bad news was no-one had paid the bill for some years and it was about as useless as an old soup can attached to a piece of string coming out of the wall.

Captain Rose charged from room to room, floorboards creaking, with William in tow.

'I can't work it out,' he said when they came back downstairs. 'You saw them? Bunks, tables, chairs. Why would someone just up and leave?'

William didn't have an answer for that. He surveyed the 'wanted' posters on the lounge room wall. They looked like Nazis and bushrangers. 'What is this place?'

Captain Rose shook his head. 'The island wasn't on our charts, so I haven't got a clue.'

'Outside might offer some clues.'

This time Captain Rose followed William out the door.

What they found 40 or 50 yards from the house only deepened the mystery.

They exchanged glances when they saw the four tombstones and a rustic wooden bench.

'Don't ask me.' William shrugged.

'Well, I don't like it.'

'We haven't got much choice but to get used to it. But look on the bright side. They can't put you in jail for having counterfeit money if you haven't got it any more. And I've managed to throw Benny and Luigi, and Wacko Jacko off my trail.'

Captain Rose frowned. 'Who's Wacko Jacko?'

'I'll have years here to fill you in.'

The captain rose to his full height, and a look of disgust came in his eyes. 'What are you suggesting? That we stay here? This dump is giving me the creeps already.'

'I can actually see real potential here. I feel I've landed on my feet.' William pointed to the horizon. 'Most of my problems have just sailed away.' His hamstring felt like it was on the mend. For the first time in days, he actually felt happy. He looked towards the house. 'What's say we let bygones be bygones and try to fix the place up? You can even have your own veggie patch.'

'You really are nuts.' Captain Rose's face contorted into a sneer.

'No, I'm not.' William laughed. 'If you give me a chance, you'll find I am a very forward-thinking, liberal-minded fellow who does a bit of magic to break the monotony of life. I can actually be very entertaining.'

'You're kidding me, right?' Captain Rose stared down into his face. 'You've already started cackling like an old man. I've seen forward-thinking liberal-minded young men fall into the same trap. It's different with women as they become older. They become more concerned with things like the environment and social justice. But blokes? We just become more cranky, more narrow-minded, more right-wing, more bigoted and a lot more twisted. Is that how you see your future?'

'I think you're exaggerating.' William grinned widely.

'Well, don't expect me to hang around. No booze, no ciggies, no casinos, no lonely rich divorcees.' Captain Rose turned and headed back to the dinghy on the beach.

William called after him. 'Where are you going?'

Captain Rose turned his head as he walked. 'You seem to forget I actually know where that ship is going.'

The last William saw of him, he was furiously paddling towards the horizon.

William was quite happy living alone here for the next 43 years, growing the legend of a hermit named Mad Bill.

That tranquility ended the day someone knocked on his door.

But that's a story for the next book in the series.

NEXT IN THE SERIES

If you enjoyed this novel and wonder where it's all leading, you won't want to miss the next in the series.

Mad Bill just wants to be left alone on his island in. So why does he make it so hard for anyone to leave?

Most of the madcap action takes place on a mysterious island off Australia where the British military used to do secret things, and left behind things like bully beef, "wanted" posters and Mad Bill's shotgun.

BUY IT

FREE EXCERPT

CHAPTER 1: SWIMMING FOR HIS LIFE

A TATTOOED ARM reached down from the back of the boat. 'Give me your hand, you stupid surfer.'

Ralph was hauled up and dumped face down on the deck.

He spat out a mouthful of sea-water on the black rubber matting, and gasped: 'Am I glad you came along?'

'What were you even thinking?' the voice above him snapped. 'You should know better at your age! You're more likely to be ripped apart by a White Pointer than catch a good wave in this bay.'

When Ralph lifted his head, the first thing he saw was the gruff man's yellow rubber boots.

When he rolled over, he saw lots of cray pots, nets and hooks. Then he spied a wheelbarrow further up the fishing boat.

The tattooed man's yellowness didn't end with his rubber boots. He was wearing yellow rubber trousers that went all the way to his armpits. He had muscular arms like Popeye, but they were much more heavily tattooed than simple anchors.

Water dripped from Ralph's clothes as he got on to his knees. As he scrambled to his feet, the whistle around his neck swung and glinted in the sun before flopping back on to the front of his soggy red-and-black striped shirt. The man facing him had the beginnings of a beard, and he reeked of fish.

Ralph pointed to the shore, which was getting smaller. 'I'm not a bloody surfer! Can't you see I'm a referee? I was chased into the bay by a mob who were unhappy with one of my decisions.' He pointed with a trembling finger. 'If I hadn't swum from the soccer field at the edge of the bay there, I'd probably be dead now.'

The boat was leaving the shelter of the bay. The wind was freshening and waves were becoming bigger. Ralph grabbed a rail as the boat rocked and rolled.

Popeye stooped down and picked up a towel, which he threw so Ralph could dab his face dry. He should have looked at it first though. Dried fish entrails taste terrible and the taste just gets worse as they rehydrate. He clenched his eyes shut and made a raspberry sound as he blew through his lips.

The shock of his hand being gripped made him open his eyes and remove the towel from his line of vision.

Popeye smiled as he squeezed Ralph's hand like it was some kind of pain-threshold test, and he shouted above the wind and the chug of the engine. 'You'll get used to swallowing a few fish guts. I'm Davy.'

'Ralph.' He was glad when his hand was released, and he saw he still had all his fingers.

Davy was about his age (the wrong side of thirty) and height (only two or three inches short of six foot) but with hands the size of buckets.

'You're come aboard *The Good Lady*.' Davy began to laugh. 'The skipper's wife thinks he named this tub after her.'

'I won't tell her otherwise. If you just take me back to shore, I'll be on my way.' When he saw that Davy's facial expression had turned dark again, Ralph added hastily: 'Of course, I'll pay you for your troubles.'

Davy spat over the side. 'It ain't up to me. I'm just the lead deckhand on this trawler. You'll have to talk to the skipper.'

Davy pointed to a raised cabin. 'You'll find Hendrik in the wheelhouse, but I've never known him to go back so soon. We usually only return when we have a full load of fish in the hold.'

'How long does that take?'

'Depends. Could be as much as two or three weeks.'

'I can't wait that long!' Ralph cried. 'People will be worried about me.'

Davy spat again. This time his green phlegm teetered on the top of the rail. Ralph didn't have to stare at it for long because a wave crashed up and swept it away.

Davy shrugged. 'Hendrik has a two-way radio in the wheelhouse, which means he can tell the authorities on shore you're safe. Sooner or later he's going to have to do the same for our two other hitchhikers.'

Ralph stretched his eyes wide: 'You mean I'm not the only one?'

BUY IT TO KEEP READING

ABOUT THE AUTHOR

John Martin is an Australian. He used to be a
journalist, now he's free to be frivolous.

https://johnmartin-author.blog

\

MY BOOKS

Windy Mountain series

Lie of the Tiger (#1)

He's not who he says he is. Who will rescue him?

———

Blokes on a Plane (#2)

Why is the mayor speaking old English? And where has he disappeared to?

———

Whitey and the Six Dwarfs (#3)

Troupe of Elvis impersonators come to the rescue.

———

Blokes in Donegal (#4)

Three old blokes go to Ireland hoping to discover family history. The mayor had to take his great, great, great grandfather's head, didn't he!

———

Blokes in the House (#5)

How the old blokes coped with COVID quarantine (clue: the major didn't).

―――

Who Knew Tasmanian Tigers Eat Apples. (#6)

Back to before the beginning. Wish-Wash leads a public revolt.

———

Who Knew Tiger Sharks also Eat Apples? (#7)

A character from the old days returns in an unlikely guise. It's all about comic revenge.

———

The Life and Deaths of Billy Gumboots (#8)

'His foot, my boot.'

———

Blokes Send in the Clones (#9)

Two old blokes have a crack at cloning a Tasmanian tiger.

To come:

10 — Blokes do the Block

Someone marries, someone dies. Might even be the same old bloke.

———

Funny Capers DownUnder series

The Wrong Magician (#1)

This time he has to make himself disappear.

———

Daddy's Great Escape (#2)

If Mad Bill hates people so much, why does he make it so hard for them to leave his island?

———

Escape from Mad Bill's Island (#3)

He came seeking to find out what the British were up to on the island in World War 2. He won't like the answer.

———

Standalone novels

Major B.S. comes to the end of his Rope

It all started when he rescued the wrong group of people from a prisoner-of-war camp. It just becomes worse.

———